DECEPTION

Mary Jay

ISBN: 978-1-909163-22-5

Fantastic Books Publishing

Cover Design by Paula Ann Murphy

License Notes

Contents

Chapter 1

The College

The painting is enigmatic; a cool, uncluttered interior with an absence of figures, doors opening to reveal glimpses of a passageway and entrances to unseen rooms. The muted palette of greys, creams and soft sepia is calming yet at the same time oddly haunting. Lines, light and colour have made up this painting. The open doors and suggestions of further interiors are ambiguous and leave many questions unanswered.

The paintings of Vilhelm Hammershoi really do have meditative qualities, Miranda considered as she drew her gaze away from the painting to the reality of the room around her. Warm, late afternoon July sun filtered through the stained glass windows of the Victorian building, casting streams of coloured light on to the canvases lined against the white washed walls. The end of year exhibition of work by the foundation course students was to be held next week and Miranda had her usual anticipation that was part excitement and part fear. The chosen theme was a 'Sense of Place' and she had attempted to inspire her students to create their own individual responses, drawing on personal experiences and, most crucially, imagination. This was not just about landscapes and physical spaces but as much about places generated by the creative powers of the mind. Recognising the need for a wide range of stimuli she had introduced them to an extensive variety of artwork, from classical drawings, painterly landscapes and gritty urban scenes to the exotic and the magical. She had made sure to include in this the Nordic artists she so much admired, Hammershoi and Munch, which were the focus of her own study for her MA. She could see in the paintings of Munch the underlying influence of the Gothic genre and had sought to make this connection in her analysis of his work. By sharing her personal obsession with her students she hoped to gain another dimension from their reactions to the artist.

Letting her gaze wander around the room, her eyes fell on Joel. It was rare for Miranda to find a student who would not respond to her positive methods but it irked her to admit that in the past year she felt she had not made enough progress with Joel; a brooding, uncommunicative young man who never smiled or engaged in the heated discussions, complaints or lively banter which characterised the interaction of the group.

As with any other student, Miranda had tried hard to get through to Joel. As part of their contact time with students, tutors had regular one to one sessions. Miranda welcomed this opportunity to get to know them better, to find out what interested them and to encourage their specific talents. She was not judgemental and was prepared to search for qualities in everyone. But with Joel it was particularly difficult. He was reluctant to release any information about himself and was usually passive in their discussions, showing little enthusiasm for their current project. He was a student who was difficult to like and Miranda wondered why he had chosen this course of study demanding energetic creativity and enthusiasm when he appeared to have little of either.

And then, Miranda discovered while looking through his portfolio that he had a real talent for portraiture. There were a number of drawings, some mere sketches and others well-defined portraits that demonstrated his acute powers of observation and ability to capture mood. This was what she had been looking for; an area of talent where she could honestly praise him. When she singled out some of these pieces for positive comment she saw a change in him; his face was more animated and she noticed that he was blushing. Although he still refused to be drawn into any real conversation he established the habit of quietly leaving drawings on her desk, and by some sort of unspoken agreement she returned them with constructive comments, praising him on his powers of observation. She was careful not to draw the attention of the rest of the group and in this way she hoped to build his confidence.

Almost as if he was aware of her thoughts he raised his head from his work and looked directly at her. It was very unusual for him to make direct eye contact, and, instead of shifting his gaze immediately as she would have expected, he allowed his eyes to linger on her in a way that made her feel distinctly uncomfortable.

After the students had collected their portfolios and left the room, the art room door clicked gently and Anni appeared, lounging casually against the lintel.

'Wine bar when you finish?'

'Yeah, sure, looking forward to it. See you there later.'

Anni was a tutor of life drawing, in her mid-thirties and several years older than Miranda; she was attractive in a sixties flower power way with loose garments, mussed up curly dark hair and a plethora of jangling cheap bracelets. She smoked tiny French cigarettes in a casually sophisticated manner that reminded Miranda of Sally Bowles in 'Goodbye to Berlin'. But Miranda knew that Anni's laid-back appearance and manner belied an anxious personality as she struggled to reconcile herself to an acrimoniously failed marriage and a need to manage independently. She worked part-time in a gift store at

Camden Lock but was trying to re-establish herself in her professional career. They had met in the store which Miranda occasionally patronised as it was near her flat in Camden Town and Miranda had introduced her to the Art College where she now offered regular life drawing sessions. Very different in appearance to Miranda with her spiky dark red hair and liking for white, grey and taupe clothing, they shared similar attitudes and ideas and could spend relaxing evenings in each other's company. When they first met Miranda had felt that here was a real soulmate. Conversation was easy and open and they now frequently met for a drink, often with other friends that Miranda had made in Camden Town, or spent cosy evenings with a bottle of wine in Miranda's flat. Anni was relaxed in her attitude to social life, often available spontaneously for a meeting and adaptable to whatever came up, whether it was a Sunday walk in the park or Saturdays spent browsing the markets. There was an unspoken feeling of connection between them that suggested something deeper.

The late May sunshine was all-embracing as Miranda left the college entrance behind the Euston

Road, which seemed a world away from the manic hustling crowds at St Pancras and the never ending noise and fumes. Here a labyrinth of narrow pedestrian streets circled between the mellow yellow brick of early twentieth-century Peabody accommodation and purpose built concrete blocks of flats erected by Camden Council in the nineteen seventies. Window boxes and pots on balconies mingled with washing lines, children's toys, bicycles; all the paraphernalia of everyday life lived in restricted urban surroundings. Grassy areas, tiny parks and playgrounds punctuated the residential blocks, adding colour with white and pink lavatera growing profusely in tiny patches of earth. Round every corner there seemed to be an Irish pub with vastly overdone hanging baskets.

She was late in leaving college this Friday (a day when staff and students traditionally made a hasty exit) and was suddenly surprised to see the lone figure of Joel walking with little sense of purpose away from the building. She knew that he lived in one of the nearby concrete blocks and had sometimes seen him in one of the park areas, occasionally lounging on the grass with a book but more often just hanging around observing the scene. She was aware that his father had recently died and had sympathy for his mother, an earnest woman desperately trying to provide for Joel and his younger brother. No doubt the lack of a father and the need to offer emotional support to his mother accounted for his apparent melancholy.

Something must have alerted him to her presence on the steps of the college because he turned abruptly and seemed about to come towards her but, after a brief hesitation, swung round without acknowledging her and walked away. Miranda was uneasy; he had wanted to approach her but something had held him back. Why? She felt strangely disturbed, and wondered again about the reasons for his isolation from the other students. And why was he waiting, apparently deliberately, when virtually everyone else had left? She had an unpleasant feeling that he was watching her.

Camden Town

Miranda's flat was the third floor of a converted Victorian terrace in Camden Town. A flight of stone steps led past a wrought iron, railed basement to what had once been an imposing front door. The building was just on the right side of neglect, with plaster work and rendering chipped and flaking in places. Her flat was up four short flights without a lift but once there she had the luxury of light, high ceilings, large windows and a feeling of space. It was a cheap conversion with only rudimentary modifications to the interior, which had the virtue of retaining some delightful original features, such as the leaded ebony jet fireplace, stripped pine floors and doors, and a sash window overlooking the street. Miranda used the main room as a living area and studio, opting for stark white paintwork relieved by framed posters and prints. She had furnished this area very simply with a battered leather settee, a round table with bentwood chairs, and a rattan coffee table with basket chairs. She had bought a large oak table which provided space for her laptop and drawing materials. It fitted in an alcove created by the fireplace wall where the shelves above it stored her files and art books. Old theatre programmes created a collage on the surround of the leaded fireplace. But her prized possession was an old chaise longue which she had had recovered in a deep caramel coloured fabric.

Drawings scattered over the table showed sketches for the piece she was currently working on; a type of contemporary triptych of a Renaissance-type doorway and arches which could have had a Venetian or Florentine influence. All her present work reflected her fascination with the architecture of romantic buildings; arches, doorways, cloisters, pillars.

Miranda recognised here possibly a desire to find something; this predilection for doorways and entrances suggesting possibilities and the chance of exciting finds and new discoveries. 'Liminal': this was the word she had encountered in her reading on the Gothic genre.

By the window hung a print of Munch's 'Vampire'. Since seeing a version of the original painting in an exhibition, Miranda had been intrigued by the motive and meaning behind the picture of the sensual woman with streaming red hair biting (or kissing?) the neck of the man she was embracing. She often found herself looking intently at the painting and trying to work out the story behind it and the intention of the artist. Presumably it wasn't meant to be attractive but it was fascinating and did make her feel excited in a strange, inexplicable way.

Three steps down from the living area led to a narrow galley kitchen with a small fire escape balcony where Miranda had placed pots of red and white begonias. The bedroom had less light than the other areas, with a window overlooking the garden area behind the house. Miranda had made her major purchases for this room with a wrought iron bed and an old dresser with an antique mirror.

A brilliantly coloured Chinese hanging bought from Church Street market hung on the wall behind the bed and a wall to ceiling row of narrow shelving held paperback novels and many of the 'found' objects that she acquired for her artwork; shells, pebbles, bits of driftwood, pieces of glass.

The feeling of pleasure at entering this space where she had created her own private haven never diminished, particularly at these exhausting moments. But all she wanted this evening was a rapid shower to cleanse the city grime before the Friday night wind down at the local wine bar.

When she arrived back at the flat after college she would sometimes encounter Julian who lived in the basement. He was self-employed as a provider of help with all domestic tasks for those whose lives were too busy and simply wanted someone to take care of cleaning, house-sitting, shopping, collecting dry cleaning, etc. He seemed busy so there must be a pretty big number of 'time poor', financially well off people out there, Miranda considered. He was an attractive looking guy and, at first, Miranda had wondered about possibilities, but after getting to know him better she understood that he was a complete control freak. They maintained a friendly, neighbourly relationship, having a drink out together occasionally, and he was very helpful about carrying stuff upstairs for her. He was, unfortunately, extremely interested in the lives of others and regarded it as his right to know everything that happened in the building.

Other occupants of the house included two Vietnamese students who shared a double bedsit. They were both well-groomed young men and nodded politely when they saw Miranda. One of the smaller rooms at the back of the house was occupied by mad Dave. He was a startling figure; skinny and dressed totally in tight-fitting black with long tangled black hair: he had an unbearably pale face and walked around hunched over listening to his iPod. He worked as a kitchen porter in a Camden restaurant and cycled to work in the evenings. In the day he could be seen wandering back from shopping trips carrying plastic carrier bugs bulging with six packs and very little indication of any form of nutrition. Miranda privately referred to him as 'the heroin addict' and would have worried that he was starving himself except she guessed he probably economised by eating in the restaurant kitchen.

A languorous girl with long blonde hair called Leila lived in the flat opposite Miranda's. She came from an affluent home in the Home Counties and was attempting to find work as a model in London. She looked the part but seemed mainly to be investing money in modelling courses and surprisingly, considering her aspirations, chose to return to her parents' home most weekends.

In the larger garden flat at the back of the house, with French windows opening on to the garden, were Mary and Elton, a warm-hearted Afro-Caribbean couple who chatted freely and were very welcoming, inviting Miranda to visit them the day she moved in. Mary was a born-again Christian and spent much of her time at prayer meetings and related social gatherings. She worked locally on the checkout in Sainsbury's and found the work tiring and caused her back problems. She had tried to coax some life out of the back garden, which, like the gardens in many multi-occupied houses, tended to be ignored. Elton had created a small patio outside their French doors and she had planted colourful plants in shrubs and had mown a small section of grass which marked an area of control before the tangled shrubbery and overhanging trees took over.

The Wine Bar

The buzz of Friday night early doors drinkers welled out of 'Le Cigale' as Miranda pushed her way through the pavement smokers. She could see Anni with a couple of other colleagues from the Art School and a number of people that Miranda met with in a nearby studio. The studio was a converted shed, owned by Rebecca, a generous, philanthropical woman who wanted to share her passion for art with like-minded people and invited a small group to use her studio as their base. Here they could paint, draw, sculpt, shared expertise and ideas and, sometimes more importantly, provide a refuge from the pressures of family, lovers and work. The peace of this artists' working environment was almost monastic and for Miranda it was an opportunity to work on large canvases and create small artefacts which she eventually hoped to sell. Much as Miranda enjoyed and was stimulated by her tutoring job, her real desire was to establish herself as a working, self-sufficient artist.

As Miranda took the first sip of the fridge-cold, Italian white wine she instantly relaxed into a sensation of freedom and lack of responsibility. Fingers sliding round her neck and down the back of her loose T-shirt made her feel charged with electricity and the feeling of anticipation associated with any meeting with Mike. She had met Mike during an animated Friday night party where he had taken her over, monopolised her fragmented attempts at conversation and had then taken her back to her flat with the promise that they could have 'something good going for them'.

He was a mountain climber and his only reason for working was to gain money to fund his passion. He currently worked as a house painter while preparing for an expedition to Patagonia where with another climber he was going to attempt the 1,400 metre North Pillar.

Miranda had responded to his insistent dominant attitude and found something darkly seductive, if slightly scary, about being with someone who was so sure of himself. There was an element of excitement if not something implicitly disquieting about their relationship. He could be excellent, entertaining company but was impatient with the trivia of everyday mundanity and claimed that once you had spent time on top of a mountain you began to despise the small-minded attitude of most people.

He had explained to her when they met that it was more about the journey than the destination, although that did provide the ultimate climax.

'When you arrive at the point where you can't go down, can't fall off and only go up suddenly it becomes very pure.'

He created evocative pictures of the climbing experience. 'It's a totally awesome sensation in the darkness; it's super intense.' Naturally she was interested in the fear element. 'You don't give in to it, you rationalise it,' he said.

By the time they left the party she was sliding into the woozy side of tipsy and actually found it very easy to be with someone who took charge and made instant decisions. He didn't interrogate her with questions about her own life but, by his attitude, vaguely suggested that he knew as much as he needed to, and that he saw her as clever, attractive and desirable.

The day after they met Mike arrived unannounced at her flat with a posy of spring flowers (which she later discovered he had picked from a nearby garden) and stated that he would take her out that evening to see a French film. (No questions asked about whether Miranda was free and wanted to go.) There was definitely something attractive in this approach and the concept of being organised and told what to do. The film was at an art house cinema where the patrons were able to take drinks from a bar into the auditorium; too sophisticated for coke and popcorn.

In an Italian pizzeria afterwards she was too animated to eat, fascinated by Mike's conversation and his totally easy attitude. The next evening when she was preparing for college her phone buzzed with a text.

'can u b ready by 9?'

There were no polite opening formalities with Mike. They got straight into conversation as they walked around the back streets of Camden to an unknown location (unknown to Miranda that was).

'What is this place?' She asked as they went into a converted Edwardian terrace and climbed dimly lit stairs to a landing.

'It's a private club, you know, the kind of place that's not publicised. You have to know it exists to find it.'

One of the nondescript doors off the landing opened into a place that could have been someone's front room except that it was packed with people. The decor was minimalist apart from stills from films and posters decorating the walls, and people were standing or sitting drinking at wooden tables. Two inappropriately glitzy chandeliers cast shadowy light over the room and Jimmy Hendrix was playing. Mike seemed to know a few of the people there and they talked over the noise of the music, drank strong lager and finally gave in to the noise so when others began to dance they joined them. The experience was somehow surreal and the next morning she would have thought that she had dreamt it except for the unpleasant evidence of a headache and a slightly queasy feeling. At college the next morning, one of her colleagues, Jasmin, looked at her rather strangely.

'Are you OK, you look a bit kind of ill?'

'Yeah, I do feel a bit queasy but it'll go. I'm afraid I went out with my new guy last night and got a bit wrecked.'

'You mean you were drunk?'

Jasmin's tone wasn't so much disapproval as non-comprehension. Jasmin was a practising Muslim and had never drunk any alcohol. Miranda felt slightly embarrassed.

'Yeah, 'fraid so. Sorry, I know it's not what you do. We live in the same world but we don't in a way.'

Although since Mike had appeared in her life, Miranda didn't even think she was living in her own world.

Since then they had spent many nights in her flat, lovemaking was frenetic and Miranda felt that he had really brought her to life. If Mike couldn't sleep he would go for long late-night walks and she became accustomed to waking to find that he was absent.

Their relationship of six months had continued in this way; spontaneous, often stimulating but equally often she was annoyed, irritated by his unwillingness to plan, occasional unreliability and his skill at wiping away discontent with his charisma.

He made it clear that his true commitment was to his climbing and, despite his contempt for the routine lives of most people, she was quickly aware that he was only able to pursue his worthy ideals by willingly accepting the generosity of others. In social situations he was an undoubted asset and she felt that she was drawn to him because of the opportunity to experience vicarious danger.

Everything with Mike had been spontaneous and uninhibited: she had met him when she was in a floaty, wine-induced haze and this semi-real aura seemed to have characterised most of their time together. Like many people who engage in extreme and hazardous sports, Mike liked to play hard. When he was climbing he was organised, disciplined and meticulous, able to endure pain and hardship without complaint. When he was not engaged in serious climbing, he was gregarious, outspoken and enjoyed sociable drinking. He had taken Miranda for some lengthy walks and had introduced her to climbing walls as a leisure activity. Spending days with Mike tended to involve strenuous, sometimes nerve wracking experiences but the reward was an animated evening and a casual approach to arrangements that could create an excited anticipation. Mike's craving for exercise never seemed to be satisfied: he ran, cycled, did kick boxing and body combat, and was always ready for more. Sometimes on Sunday mornings when they had spent Saturday night together he would go out for a long run or cycle ride while Miranda caught up on lazy sleep after the rigours of the week. Returning in the middle of the morning when Miranda was showered and reading the papers, they would breakfast together on coffee and fresh croissants that Mike had bought on the way back, and then he would begin planning activities for the rest of the day. After a complete day in Mike's company when they had been walking or working out in the park, Miranda just needed some rest before they set out for the evening. She loved these times when Mike would join her and they would make love and then she would drift, exhausted, into soothing dreams while recharging her energies for the night ahead.

With the wine bar conversation increasingly loud and energetic, and the wine and beer flowing, they ordered the wine bar's self-styled 'tapas' which were platters of cheese, bread, salami and olives.

Looking round the group Miranda felt contented and reassured to be among interesting, like-minded people, to consider her pleasure at her students' preparation for their exhibition and to reflect on her plans for her own work. By 11.30 pm she was suddenly overcome with tiredness and the need to get back to the privacy of her flat where she could think about ideas for her work in progress before retreating to bed. She refused Mike's offers of a walk home and drifted quietly back with her mind buzzing with creative ideas. The streetlight at the end of her road had been defunct for some time so she turned the corner into a patch of darkness. There seemed to be someone sitting on the steps outside her house and as she got closer she could discern a thin, young male figure. Surely, it couldn't be ... an unpleasant sensation swept away her inebriated feeling as she considered the possibility that it might be Joel. Her students knew that she lived in Camden and some had been to the flat to drop off work, so it wouldn't have been difficult for him to find out; but as she got near a familiar voice interrupted her thoughts.

'Hi Mandy.'

It was her younger brother Toby, nineteen and living at their parental home in Sheffield. He'd dropped out of his college music course and moved from temporary jobs in bars, coffee shops and places where students could find work.

'Toby; great, but why?'

'Hope it's OK but need somewhere to crash for a bit. Had a bit of a bust-up with Mum and Dad so need to keep out of their way for a while.'

'OK, I'm desperate for bed so let's go in and sort you out while you tell all. Oh, where's your stuff?'

'Ah, that's something else; Jenny's with me and she's got the bags. She wanted to wait in the back garden while I sussed out how you'd feel. Thing is, she's pregnant and that's the reason for the row, so if we could both stay till I get it sorted we'd just love you forever.'

As Toby appeared from the garden with Jenny and two huge backpacks, Miranda envisaged her lovely private space now being invaded by Toby and Jenny and their belongings.

Toby had frequently stayed over and she enjoyed his company but never with a pregnant Jenny, which would certainly alter circumstances. It would seem that both sets of parents had blown up at the news, deploring the potential waste of Jenny's ambitions to go to university as she was currently taking her A levels. Jenny's parents were relatively affluent and her mother, who exerted much control over Jenny, had immediately offered to organise and pay for a termination so she could continue her studies without interruption.

Having never totally approved of Toby, or his family, she had assumed that this would signal the end of the relationship. But that hadn't been Toby and Jenny's plan: they wanted to have the baby and Toby intended to seek better paid work while Jenny completed her studies. Miranda's parents had also been unforgiving and had adopted a strong moral line. Miranda couldn't decide whether she admired Toby and Jenny for their determination to get through this together or felt worried for them at their naive Romeo and Juliet attitude. But she definitely wasn't sure about having them invade her personal space. There was a tiny box room next to Miranda's bedroom which she used on occasions when friends stayed the night. It was furnished in a rudimentary way with a futon, a clothes rail and a painted storage chest. She had been considering the possibility of making it more habitable so that she could make some money by subletting to foreign students who would require only short-term accommodation. That was where they would have to stay. Many possible questions and problems crossed Miranda's mind but she was too tired and it was far too late to delve into those issues now.

Since moving to London Miranda had had minimal contact with her parents. She loved them and could see their qualities but found their implied and overt criticism of her lifestyle just too oppressive at times.

Miranda's parents lived in cheerful, struggling middle-class austerity. Although apparently unconventional they were in fact very rigid in their ideas. Her father had a small furniture making and repair business which he ran from workshops in their back garden. Her mother, who had trained professionally as a dancer, had taught dance classes for many years (a job she had been able to combine with bringing up a family) and although she was no longer physically fit enough herself to teach, she was still able to arrange classes and hire teachers to work for her. She had once been attractive and vivacious but in middle age had become very overweight and was permanently on a diet. Her system for dieting, however, was to prepare substantial meals for family and friends, eating almost nothing herself at the dining table and then punctuating the day with regular trips to the kitchen to snack on treats she had stored up; the fridge contained smoked salmon ribbons, chocolate ice cream and mini chocolate bars. The logic being that if it didn't go on to a plate, and she wasn't actually sitting down, it didn't count as eating. Eva had studied English literature and her romantic element was shown in her naming of Miranda and Toby after Shakespearean characters.

Visits home usually began well with pleasant conversation over a leisurely meal discussing family issues, but the atmosphere could rapidly deteriorate into an interrogation of Miranda about her work, her flat and her social life. Miranda only ever presented edited versions of these aspects of her life and had not acknowledged the existence of Mike as she knew they would want to meet him. Bringing Mike to meet her parents wouldn't work as it would lead to endless questioning about their relationship and the old disapproval of her behaviour would surface again.

Camden Town

Sometimes Miranda thought that Saturday morning was the best time of the week as she started her morning run to Camden Lock and its environs. Early morning places held a fascination for her; a sense of secret pleasure at being one of the few people around before the noise, tumult and general chaos of big city life took hold. She savoured the quiet streets and brief encounters with familiar figures. The tall, fit looking guy who emerged from a door at the side of the newsagent's to walk his two German Shepherds (they exchanged nods of recognition; she'd never spoken to him but had overheard the newsagent calling him Rob). Then there was the elderly road sweeper on the High Street who regularly shouted 'hello, sugar,' as she passed. Even the drop out who persistently asked her for money although she repeatedly assured him that she didn't have/would never have any.

She looked with distaste at the Friday night refuse strewn over the pavements but noted as she passed the open McDonald's that an attempt had been made to clear up: she remembered being told by a student who worked for one of the franchises that employees were encouraged to collect any litter with the company logo. Further back from the High Street there were small galleries, smarter boutique style shops and quirky design and gift shops. She occasionally slowed down to glance in the windows of some of them on her return journey, hoping to glean creative ideas.

Once getting into her run she enjoyed the rhythmic movement of her feet making contact with the pavement, remembering to pull in abdominals and tightening upper thigh muscles. As she ran she would project her thoughts into the day ahead, things that needed to be done, anything she was looking forward to, and she made mental lists. She ran a couple of miles and then towards the end walked briskly, savouring the delightful heart-pounding sensation. The flower seller near the station had set out her stall; this was Miranda's personal timing device; she always knew she was late home from college if the flower stall was closed.

She considered how later in the day this place was so different; a complete hustle of noise, smells and activities. Tattoo parlours, shops selling incense and crystals for healing, bikers in their leathers and dramatic Goths with their multiple piercings, thick white pan-stick and purple barbed wire bracelets. (Where do these people live and work or do they just emerge during the day as if part of a stage set? Miranda often wondered.) The plethora of cafes and bars, some second hand bookstores and self-styled 'antique' shops that Miranda frequently checked out for bargains when setting up her flat, like the shop owned by the Egyptian art dealer with a crazy chaos of paintings, mirrors and wood block prints crammed into the shop and spilling out on to the pavement. The shop looked like a total jumble but was well worth excavating; it was here on one of her forays that Miranda had discovered the print of Munch's 'Vampire'.

Jammed in between two stalls selling cheap and expensive tat was Neil's vintage record and clothing store. Neil was an ardent fan of Marianne Faithful and sat at the rear of the narrow store on a deckchair looking out through a French window on to a neglected courtyard. He sometimes saved pieces that he thought Miranda would like: sixties' bags and jewellery, and ex-Biba sweaters. She liked to call in here just for a chat.

Once back at the flat Miranda showered, collected her portfolio and set off for Rebecca's studio. The Studio

Rebecca lived in a tall, three-storey renovated Victorian semi with a long sheltered back garden. It was here that she had converted a garden shed into a working studio for her group to meet. The smell of roasting coffee greeted Miranda and she felt ready to start work. Some of the others were already there and working on their individual projects, ranging from large canvases and sculptures to more precise miniatures and watercolours. Rebecca was working on a Mediterranean-inspired view stimulated by her regular foreign travels. She painted methodically and with an easy grace which Miranda found inspiring, if a little daunting to watch. All the group members were supportive, encouraging and amusing company when they relaxed over coffee breaks but Miranda's favourite was Max, a rather aristocratic older guy who reminded her of an ageing Sebastian Flyte.

Max was a talented painter and sculptor who enjoyed the challenge of producing spontaneous works. He sometimes asked Miranda very courteously, if she would sit for him while he drew her. He claimed that her face reminded him of Rita Tushingham in 'A Taste of Honey' and he usually affectionately referred to her as 'Tush'.

Rebecca's studio was a large, wooden shed-like structure with a pitched roof and big windows on two sides. The room was invariably cold and was heated by paraffin heaters: some of the group wore hats and many wore fingerless gloves, which gave them a rather raffish appearance. Roseanne, who was generously built with long curly blonde hair and a flawless skin, was usually draped in scarves in soft pastel shades.

As soon as she came into the studio Miranda felt she was entering a special place. Despite the chill and the odour of paraffin, she felt embraced by the sight of the canvases, paints and easels, the rich aroma of percolating coffee and the easy, relaxed friendliness of the others. With the caffeine hit of her first coffee she felt slightly giddy and she knew that she was ready to start work.

As part of her zeal to promote the group's work Rebecca had introduced them to the owners of a small private gallery in Camden selling contemporary art and sculpture. Kate and Paul were smart young entrepreneurs who were willing to exhibit the work of aspiring artists and they had offered the group the opportunity of a private view. This was scheduled for the weekend after Miranda's end of term which coincided with her birthday, and any spare time she could find was now devoted to finishing her exhibition piece of the triptych. Her interest in Renaissance and Medieval buildings was apparent in the work and she frequently referenced the drawings and sketches of Ruskin and Palladio.

What she was attempting to create were images which would draw in the viewer and allow them to imagine hidden and secret places. She was interested in the blurring of boundaries between supernatural and illusory dimensions, and the shifting of rational structures. Her current work featured arches, columns, decaying structures, cloisters and subterranean vaults: the type of buildings that excited and confused, that suggested duplicity and ambiguity. Her work space was filled with her reference material:

preparatory sketches in charcoal, architectural drawings (some by Palladio), photographs she had taken on holidays in Italian cities, pieces of fabric in appealing colours and even literature. Initial sketching was an important part of her process and she often thought of the words of her favourite tutor who emphasised the significance of 'making marks on paper'. Her drawings were loyal to this method, working with pencil, graphite and charcoal she made ever-deepening straight and cross-hatched lines to create shapes and the illusion of space.

As she set to work Miranda could feel her creative energies soaring. She worked with mixed media, using candle wax and chalk on the base of the canvas, painting with pastels and incorporating tiny pieces of antique lace and silver paint to represent decorative work. On good days like this she could give way to total absorption and feel completely at one with her work.

Chapter 2

Joel

It was the countdown to the students' end of term show. With only a few days left Miranda was keen to get everyone organised so she was irritated to arrive in her work room full of ideas and energy to find that she had to motivate and encourage students who mainly seemed to have lost all desire to work, if indeed to live, after their various weekend pursuits.

But then she considered how much she had been rewarded by her students' enthusiasm in creating their own sense of place. The paintings of her most committed student filled her with pleasure: Jacob, an attractive, lively Afro-Caribbean was seriously dedicated to his art, which displayed unusual confidence for his age. He had been particularly inspired both by Chris Offili and by his own Jamaican heritage, which was all reflected in the vibrant rich colours emanating from his work.

The twins, Jessica and Francesca, attractive girls with Italian parents and hair like that of Pre-Raphaelite models, had an apparently leisurely approach to their work; confident brush strokes on large canvases and a willingness to experiment with different types of media. One that she couldn't quite come to terms with was a girl called Jude. She had commitment to her art but in a strange sort of way; unwilling to take advice and never wanting to follow the prescribed path, she produced an ill-assorted range of pieces which had no apparent personal style, and yet Miranda was convinced there was genuine talent there. Jude was always ready to challenge and, while it was undeniably good for the tutor to have a provocative element in the group, at times it was intensely irritating. Miranda also found herself having to protect Jude from the wrath of the faculty managers, who were more interested in conformity and subscribing to the party line than encouraging individuality. Jude often stayed behind after college to discuss her work and, occasionally, they would move their discussion into the student coffee bar.

But as she brought her mind back to the present she was further annoyed by the fact that someone seemed to have interfered with the materials she had so carefully sorted on her table before leaving the previous Friday. As she resorted files and note books, a piece of paper detached itself. It was a pen and ink drawing of a young woman in a dreamy, reflective pose. It looked romantic until on closer inspection Miranda noticed what appeared to be marks and scratches on the female's neck and arms. It was at the same moment that she also realised it was meant to be her. How unpleasant, that someone should have taken the time to do this and then leave if for her as a type of message.

A faculty meeting had been called for mid-morning to finalise paperwork and also arrangements for the show. It was inevitably tedious as members of the department tended to have differing views which they aired vocally. The faculty heads, Malcolm and Angela, were a brother and sister team who took an autocratic approach and looked for compliance; difficult when leading a team of creative and original people. Miranda personally felt that their influence was stifling and limited what she could achieve with her students; she also suspected that they were envious of the fact that she was a practitioner and worked with her students rather than dictating her ideas. Sue, who was thin, sharp-featured and given to almost incessant swearing, was usually able to antagonise them with her forthright, acid comments. Sue had discovered her sexuality and preference for women when she was a young teenager and she said that the fight to establish herself as a gay woman of intelligence and integrity had been a hard one, and she was not easily defeated. Susannah, however, could be relied on to provide the voice of reason and restore equilibrium to any of their more antagonistic sessions. Susannah was a Canadian who had met and married an English academic while he was on a visiting lecture post at her university. She had come back with him to the UK where they had set up home, had three children and employed a variety of foreign au pairs so that Susannah could continue with her career. Miranda had often been welcomed and entertained in Susannah's home and liked the temporary excursion into family life. Susannah was smaller and chunkier than Miranda and dressed mainly in garments purchased from designer outlets: loose dresses and long cashmere sweaters worn over black leggings with bold silver earrings.

Miranda had a sneaking affection for Justin who seemed to be a fairly complex character. In his mid-thirties he was very theatrical looking; dark-haired and with a trace of designer stubble, he dressed in smart jeans and leather blousons with a bandanna tied round his forehead. He was totally committed to his work and exacting in his standards and expectations of the students. He tended to be disregarded by the other faculty members as he wasn't a team player and avoided any contact or confrontation with the faculty heads. He spent his time in meetings saying very little and scribbling notes which in fact were design ideas for his large Georgian house which he was constantly renovating. He seemed to have an enormous number of friends from various spheres of the art world whom he entertained in his home. Unmarried, but it was rumoured via the water-cooler gossip that he lived with a very attractive older woman who owned her own business. That would account for the clothes and lifestyle that appeared extravagant for his salary. Interestingly, Justin, who appeared to be unconventional, had once warned Miranda about becoming too friendly with Jude. A short conversation had taken place one day after Justin had seen Miranda and Jude talking together in the student coffee bar.

'I'd be careful about getting too friendly with Jude. She seeks out the company of older people and she wants to be seen as mature but she's got a bit of a drink problem and there are difficulties at home. Her mother says that even the slightest suggestion of criticism or refusing to do what Jude wants inevitably leads to an explosion like the start of World War three.'

'Strange, I haven't really seen that side of her,' Miranda said. 'She can be volatile in class and there have been a few episodes of conflict with others in the group but I find that fairly typical of art students.'

'Yeah, well I'm just saying,' Justin said, and left it at that.

But the particularly fascinating staff member was the art history tutor, Jasmin Ackbar. Jasmin was a curious mixture of contradictions. She typically wore a black head covering with smart European clothes. She was soft-spoken yet able to exert a quiet authority over the students. Her family home was in Pakistan and she had arrived in the UK as a young bride with her husband who was pursuing a medical degree. Now in his final year of study, Jasmin worked to support both of them. She was therefore an independent woman in the workplace with responsibility as a provider, yet she defended the tradition of arranged marriages and the essential modesty of females. In staff room conversations she spoke with enthusiasm for the process of the arranged marriage, emphasising that her own parents were educated and liberal people who selected suitable young men to meet her but were prepared to accept her decision. There was never to be any element of compulsion. Jasmin had described to Miranda her first meeting with the man who was now her husband.

'I'd already been introduced to two guys whom I just didn't get on with and this particular day I arrived home from university for the arranged meeting with Jamal. He was already installed in the living room, being plied with cakes and tea by my mother and chatting happily with my younger sister. I was introduced and then excused myself while I took my books to my room and prepared for the evening.

Jamal talked to the family members, was invited to eat a family meal with us that evening and afterwards we talked for an hour alone. At the end of our talk he asked if I would like to meet him the next evening, and, as I said "Yes" I knew that he would be the one.'

Miranda had met Jamal as he sometimes collected Jasmin from work, mainly Miranda guessed to avoid her having to use public transport. She was prepared to travel by bus or tube at busy times of day but would not travel alone in a car with a man or take the risk of using public transport at quiet times. Jamal was a broad shouldered rather sombre man with a slightly pock-marked complexion. He was highly courteous and appeared to be a considerate, thoughtful partner. It was clear that Jasmin adored him and her expression when with him conveyed the sort of open affection that European women would have been reluctant to demonstrate. Jasmin was reserved in her language and the other team members, Sue in particular, had to apologise at times for the spontaneous use of expletives. Miranda found Jasmin's approach to life intriguing and admired the way that she managed to accommodate herself unselfconsciously to apparently disparate cultures and lifestyles.

Today Miranda was desperate for the meeting to be over so that she could return to her room. When Malcolm signalled that he had done Miranda collected her files and started back towards her room that was located at the end of the block.

The corridor, usually hard to navigate because of staff and students wandering around with portfolios, books and coffee cups, was strangely deserted for this time of day and there was no one in sight. But Miranda barely had time to consider this before she was slammed in to the wall, her files and papers fell in a heap on the floor and she could feel warm breath on her neck as Joel forced himself against her and pulled her shoulders towards him. She could feel his hands running over her body under her clothes as he pushed her against the wall. And then he was gone; the moment over as if it had never been; but it had happened and she was shaking and felt queasy. There was no time to consider what to do; she had to return to the class and suddenly, there was Jacob; fresh-faced, wholesome Jacob, picking up her things and commenting on the fact that she always rushed around carrying too much. He chatted casually as they walked back to her room together, unaware of her traumatic state. It was impossible to concentrate on what Jacob was saying and she flinched as he moved closer to her. The last thing she wanted was any possibility of body contact with anyone at the moment. She felt violated and her mind was racing ahead, wondering how she could deal with this and whom she could turn to.

In the room all the students were now working industriously, an unusually tranquil atmosphere (no doubt generated by the impending deadline) which contrasted sharply with her agitated state. She noted that Joel was not there and felt distinctly relieved. At least it would buy her some time to consider this problem that she had to resolve.

Trying to calm herself and restore normality; she toured the room, commenting on the work, responding to questions but not really listening while she tried to make sense of what had just happened. Just before the end of the session Joel appeared with an inaudible, muttered excuse. He didn't meet her gaze and gave no indication that anything had occurred; in fact, she began to wonder if it had actually happened. The session drew to a close and the last student had barely left the room as Joel walked up to her table, ostensibly to hand in his notebook but instead of leaving it on the table as she expected he walked behind her and she felt his hand sliding around her waist and then gradually moving down her legs. This couldn't be happening to her. She felt a hot flush suffuse her and instinctively she pulled away, repelled by his touch. She was finding it difficult to breath, as if something was pressing heavily on her chest; and then pure rage overcame her.

'How dare you do that? How can you assume that you can touch me? Haven't you heard of sexual harassment? Do you know the consequences of what you're doing? Don't you dare come near me or touch me ever again!'

There was no response but to her horror she realised he was crying uncontrollably.

Camden Town

Reaching Camden Town that evening Miranda felt shaky and empty. She couldn't face going straight to the flat with Toby and Jenny there, and the effort it would take to behave normally. She needed time to come to terms with what had happened and decide what to do. Sitting in Starbucks with a coffee she went over her options. Logically, she should report Joel: it was a clear case of sexual harassment. She felt soiled and violated and repulsed by the feeling that he might have actually thought she would welcome his attentions. Of all her male students, he was the one she would have defined as the least attractive, in manner, appearance and personality. She was unwilling to take this to Malcolm and Angela as she was convinced that in some way they would use this against her, perhaps by implying that her relationship with her students was too informal (she knew that they were jealous of her popularity with young people and the easy, open manner they adopted with her). Who else could she turn to for advice? Susannah would adopt a strongly feminist stance and insist that she make a formal complaint. Anni, on the other hand, with her compassionate social worker's approach, might dwell on trying to analyse why he had done it. People outside of college? Definitely not Mike, who would want to seek out Joel and beat him up. As an attractive male who never lacked female attentions, Mike wouldn't be able to imagine the narrow, isolated world that Joel seemed to inhabit.

Toby? Well, he had his own problems and would in any case make a similar response to Mike. Tell her friends at the studio? No, it was too remote from them and they might even feel sorry for her which would leave her feeling diminished. She then considered the implications of a formal report for Joel himself. He would no doubt be suspended, the effect on his recently widowed mother would be damaging, and however much she attempted to deal with it privately everyone would find out. Miranda felt vulnerable and she couldn't bear the thought of this very personal episode being publicly exposed. The only solution then would be to keep it to herself and bury it as a secret. Except, it wasn't only her secret, it was hers and Joel's.

Returning to her flat with forced cheerfulness she found Toby in the kitchen preparing kedgeree (no doubt in an attempt to placate her for having invaded her life).

'Hi Mandy, I'm doing one of your favourites, used a bit of stuff out of the cupboards but bought the fish.'

'Thanks, how's Jenny?'

'In our room; go and see how she's sorted it.'

Miranda tentatively knocked on the door to her own spare room.

'Hi! This is great, Miranda. What do you think?'

Jenny invited her in. They had risked a trip home with the help of a friend and his car to collect 'a few things'. A brightly patterned red throw was over the futon, Miranda's clothes rail was heaped with clothes, mainly Jenny's, and Toby's guitar was propped near the window. There was even a huge teddy bear resting on the pillows. This all looked far more permanent than she had anticipated. The ringing of her doorbell saved her from having to think of a response. Living three flights up it was a drag to go up and down stairs to unannounced visitors so she adopted her usual habit of leaning out of the living room window. Anybody acceptable and she would throw down the keys. It was Mike. She met him on the landing and explained about the presence of Toby and Jenny. He seemed rather unimpressed in case it interfered with their privacy but otherwise not too concerned as he was very fired up about some potential funding for his proposed Patagonia expedition. Going back into the kitchen to check with Toby that there was enough kedgeree for four, she noticed a bottle of white wine that she had left in the fridge opened on the worktop. Toby's funds had obviously not run to wine for the kedgeree so she poured herself a large glass. Sitting at the table later with Mike, Jenny and Toby, a steaming dish of fish between them and another bottle of wine that Mike had dashed out to get, as she listened to Mike's enthusiastic explanations to Toby about his climbing expedition, Jenny and Toby's gratitude for her hospitality and details of their future plans, she realised what an unpleasant intrusion into their evening her account of the Joel episode would have been. It suddenly seemed remarkably easy to pretend that nothing untoward had happened. And also she didn't even need to contribute to the conversation as no one noticed her misery. Another glass of wine helped considerably, but what she had really yearned for was to be alone with her painting and her books where she could lose herself in another world.

In the weeks that followed, Toby and Jenny established themselves in Miranda's flat. Toby quickly secured a job in a busy Weatherspoons where he met some people with similar musical interests. Jenny was more difficult to quantify and Miranda found her rather awkward to relate to. She claimed to spend her days studying but when Miranda returned in the evenings she was usually either lounging on the futon in a chaos of books and papers, listening to music in their room or sitting vaguely in the living room staring out of the window. It irritated Miranda that it never occurred to Jenny to initiate preparations for a meal or to do any cleaning. She also felt that so much time indoors and Jenny's reluctance to give up smoking was not the way to approach her pregnancy.

The Park

It was a warm Saturday morning and they were in a park in Camden Town with Mike instructing her on boxing. Mike had introduced her to this as a great way to get toned.

'And, the best part about it,' he said, 'is that you can do it outside.'

Mike was a demanding instructor and after an hour of jabs, left and right hooks and upper cuts she was glowing and exhausted and had off-loaded most of the week's accumulation of tensions. The problem of Joel seemed to have been relegated to a parallel world. She felt adrenalin surging through her and laughed as she said.

'That was great but I've had it: my legs have turned to jelly.'

'OK, that's fine,' Mike said. 'Enough for today, you can practise lunges and squats any time in the week and we'll try to fit in a session next weekend.'

They went in search of a coffee shop with newspapers where they could read and relax for a while. Finding a quiet corner with soft chairs and a low coffee table they spread out the papers.

'I'm thinking about summer holidays,' Miranda said, as she browsed through the travel section.

'OK, what do you usually do?'

'Not usually anything; more or less what turns up and what I can afford. But I've taken to European cities recently where I can look at buildings and art and get inspired. No more drunken beach parties in Ibiza.'

'Anything in mind?' Mike asked.

'Maybe. You know that guy Paulo who works in Le Cigale sometimes?'

'Think so. Do you mean the Italian?'

'Portuguese, actually; think he comes from Porto. Anyway, he's always saying what a fantastic city Lisbon is. He knows the kind of work I do and he says "Meerandaa, you should go there. You would love it." So, yeah, that's a possibility.'

'OK then. Let's go,' Mike said.

'What do you mean, let's go?'

'What does it sound like? Let us go.'

'You want to come with me?'

'Yes, good; you're getting there.'

This was unbelievable; a holiday in a European city with Mike, away from Camden Town and college and other people.

'What about your Patagonia trip?'

'Under control. I reckon I can afford a short break with my beautiful girl before setting off.'

She felt childishly excited. Already warm and pulsing from the exercise in the park she was in a semi-euphoric state. She reached over the table to hug him and then, relaxing back on to the soft leather settee she let her gaze wander over the other customers in the coffee shop. Could any of them imagine how happy she was? She was almost too nervous to look back at Mike in case it was a joke or he had changed his mind.

It turned into one of her ideal days. They walked in Regents Park, sat on the grass in the sun and talked more about Mike's expedition. They ended up in the early evening in a pub near Mike's house.

'Let's stay in tonight and I'll make something,' Mike said.

'OK, that's fine by me.'

It would be a rare pleasure; a complete leisurely evening alone without having to make conversation with friends in the wine bar or talk to waiters in restaurants or have to consider Toby and Jenny if they were in her flat. Mike was the person she most wanted to be with so that she could push to the back of her mind her revulsion at the experience with Joel.

She rarely stayed in his shared house as it was a bachelor mess squared, with four men living together. Mike's own room was preternaturally clean and tidy but was sparsely furnished, packed with climbing gear stacked against the walls, a clothes rail that served as wardrobe and shelves in an alcove wall which contained all his other possessions. Mike's motto was: 'There isn't anything that can't be carefully stacked.'

His methodical organisation didn't extend to the rest of the house which was stereotypically verging on squalor but he did engage in regular disputes with the others about kitchen cleanliness and organisation.

One of their lazy indulgences was to take food and wine up to his room and eat at a small table under the narrow window with something suitable playing on the CD. Mike's tastes were fairly retro but that evening he'd gone for an Amy Winehouse album. The powerful, languorous female voice was in tune with Miranda's mood and she considered again how lucky she was to be having a relationship with a guy as attractive as Mike. Whatever happened in the future, he had brought a real excitement into her life.

Her mobile woke her in the early hours of the morning. Caller ID: Jenny. Unusual.

'Hi, Jenny. What is it?'

'Toby hasn't come home.'

She struggled to focus on the clock: 4.00 am.

'Well, maybe he's still at the bar.'

'No, they close at 2.00 and he's always back by now. I've been trying his mobile and it's switched off. Will you help me look for him?'

'How do we look for him? We can't just wander round the streets. Perhaps he's gone to someone's place to listen to music or gone on to a late club or something. You know he does things impulsively.'

'No, he wouldn't do that. Shall we call the police?'

'He's not a missing person, Jenny; not yet anyway. They'll just tell us to wait until he's been gone for some time.'

Miranda did think that Toby was capable of spontaneously going off to a club or to spend time with people he'd met at the bar; sometimes he was incredibly vague about time and what he should be doing, but Jenny was distressed and her anxiety was becoming infectious. And she wouldn't be calmed.

'What if he's had an accident?'

'We could call the local hospitals to set your mind at rest. Do you want me to come home?'

'Yes, please.' She was crying by now.

'OK; don't know how good transport is this time of day but I'll be there as soon as I can.'

'Gotta go,' Miranda said, as she quickly explained to Mike.

'I'm coming with you.'

Back at her flat she attempted to calm Jenny who was walking around frantically smoking, having apparently forgotten Miranda's no smoking indoors rule, while Mike phoned local A & E departments: nothing, and Toby's mobile remained unobtainable.

It was 9.00 am when Toby returned, looking exhausted and edgy. He'd been picked up by police for 'a stop and search' while he was walking home and after discovering cannabis he was taken to a police cell and locked up for the night. He was furious rather than relieved.

'All I was doing was walking home with some guys from the bar when they stopped us.'

'For God's sake, Toby,' Miranda said.

'It was about a teaspoon of weed, that's all. Pity they haven't got anything better to do, like catching criminals.'

'Are they going to charge you?' Mike asked.

'No, they said that keeping me in overnight was to teach me a lesson as I only had enough for my own personal use.'

'You might at least have phoned or texted me,' Jenny complained. 'I was scared.'

'I couldn't, could I? They took everything from me, even my watch. Didn't know what time it was. And I was pretty scared as well in that god-awful cell with no idea of what was happening. They wouldn't let me call anyone; that's part of the punishment.'

'That's a violation of human rights.' Mike was angry. 'I'm going down there to sort them out. Which police station was it?'

'Leave it, Mike,' Miranda said. 'It's not worth it. They haven't charged him so it's no big deal, except we were all frantic with worry; but try to be more careful, Toby.'

'Oh, come on, you used to do stuff when you were a student. Don't think I can't remember.'

'Yeah, but I didn't get caught; and I don't want them coming round here. Did you give them this address?'

'Yeah, could hardly give our house in Sheffield. Don't want Mum and Dad in this: for all I know they might have called to check.'

'Well, watch it anyway and don't smoke the stuff here. It might not be net-curtain twitching area but some of our neighbours are nosy. Julian's made comments about the "aroma" a couple of times when he's carried things up for me.'

'Why, do you think he's a right-wing hanger and flogger?'

'Well, he does read The Telegraph, which makes him suspect.'

That defused the tension and suddenly everyone was laughing.

Chapter 3

The Studio

Her work at the studio increasingly absorbed more of Miranda's time; her students were largely in control of their end of year exhibition and she felt that she had done what she could for them; now more of her energies could be focused on her own work.

She loved the textures of the materials she was working with: the gouache, charcoal, graphite, wax and chalk, and the sheer excitement of seeing a painting taking shape. The stage she had reached with her triptych was where the work began to take on a life of its own. As she worked on the arches, pillars and delicate interstices and fragments of the building she thought of how much she wanted her audience to be as intrigued by the shapes and suggestions as she was. What she was really creating was a space for the imagination to wonder what lay behind the arches and entrances, down winding cloisters and who or what occupied the spaces. Her paintings were rather like a stage set, ready and poised for the action to begin. She wanted to unleash the imagination of the viewer and lead them into a different world.

This, she recognised was what had first attracted her to Hammershoi. Whereas she had represented her ideas via images resonant of Renaissance and classical architecture, he depicted interiors or scenes that were notable for their relative absence of people. An almost paradoxical presence was created by this absence.

Deep in thought, 'Miranda, time for you to take a break.' Her musings were interrupted by Max.

'Mind if I look?' He spent some time studying her work. 'It's good stuff.'

'Thanks, you are very encouraging but I hope that it will seem appealing once it's in a professional exhibition space. I love working on it but then when I stand back and look around the room at the works the rest of you have created it somehow seems naive and not painterly enough.'

'You don't need to torment yourself, Miranda. Avoid being too analytical and let yourself go with it.'

He leant towards her, gave her a quick hug and a kiss on the cheek.

Rebecca was clearly keen to close the studio so after a brief excursion round the room to comment on each others' work, they collected things and left. Out on the street Miranda felt the adrenalin buzz that came at the end of a concentrated session. On the way home her thoughts turned to the evening. Mike had called earlier to check if it was OK to come round. His house painting jobs tended to finish early in the day and after hours of hard physical work he was ready for relaxation, social chat and drinking. She was aware that they weren't always operating with synchronised moods these days. His concerns were more practical as hers were becoming increasingly inward focused and cerebral. For Miranda the excitement in their relationship was always there but she found it difficult to discuss her painting with Mike and for him to share her passion. She would have loved to include him in what was a very important part of her world but when she began to talk about it seriously his eyes took on a distant expression which meant he was thinking of something else (no doubt projecting into plans for his Patagonia trip). She had accepted that she couldn't push Mike into any deep discussion of her painting at this stage. Then her thoughts turned to how they would spend the evening. Take out pizzas or Chinese would fit the bill.

That was the great thing about London life; it wasn't necessary to plan and be routine; every option was available.

In the living room there was a vase of wild flowers on the table and the unmistakable smell of lasagne. Mike? Toby? Surprisingly it was Anni who emerged from the kitchen.

'Hi, I finished early today and met Mike while I was out shopping. He was getting some stuff to bring to you for tonight and I wasn't doing anything so we thought we'd combine. Lasagna and salad, and there's enough for Toby and Jenny as well.'

'Oh, great. Yes, I'm exhausted and starving so I'll shower and change. Where is Mike anyway?'

'Despatched to get some booze.'

It was pleasant to come home to a tidy flat and a meal cooking but there was something nagging uneasily at Miranda. Mike and Anni had arranged the evening to suit them without consulting her; a text while she was at the studio would at least have prepared her. She was disappointed at not having Mike to herself; since the episode with Joel she felt very vulnerable and longed for their intimate time together when she could feel attractive and wanted in a completely normal way.

He arrived while she was showering and greeted her with a towel and lingering kisses.

'God, you smell good. I have a confession to make: I had decided to look after you this evening and cook a real dish for a change but our fairy godmother appeared from nowhere in the shape of Anni and I didn't need much persuading to let her take over.'

'Mmm, I have noted the regular appearance of our fairy godmother these days.'

His face darkened slightly.

'Meaning what, exactly?'

'Well, she does seem to be around us rather a lot without a specific invitation.'

'Don't be so anal, Miranda, do you have to issue a formal invitation before you see someone?'

The last thing she wanted was to disrupt the evening and disturb their relationship so she attempted to turn her comment into a joke (although whether to convince herself or Mike she wasn't sure) and deliberately hugged him as they joined the others.

Anni had added a dressed bowl of salad leaves to the table and had found Miranda's antique looking candlesticks which now had tapers burning in them.

'Thanks, Anni. You sure are a good homemaker. This is all so inviting.'

As she accepted a glass of wine and waited to be served lasagne from the earthenware dish, Miranda reflected that this must be what having a wife was like. To arrive home dog-tired and be greeted with welcoming food and a drink poured.

Yes, she could see the attraction, but Anni did make her feel inadequate with her ability to quietly step in and take over.

All of this was good, simple and economical. In a similar situation Miranda would no doubt have resorted to good quality quick food from M & S, and consequently a hefty bill.

But supper was delightful and Mike was in an excellent mood.

During the general chat, Toby discussed his work in Wetherspoons and his ambition to develop a career in a recording studio while Jenny made arrangements to continue her studies. Money, or rather the lack of it was, as ever, the major problem.

'Well, if you'd like some extra work how about sitting as a model for a few of my life drawing classes,' Anni suggested. 'Pay's minimal but the work's easy enough, if boring. And it might suit you if you're free in the day.'

Much laughter ensued from Mike and Toby himself and Anni gently addressed Jenny.

'Are you OK with that Jenny? You do understand this is purely an artistic thing, nothing sexual about it, although I guess for my students it will make a pleasant change from the regular female model.'

If Jenny had been uncertain at the suggestion she was clearly embarrassed now and Anni's gentle, conciliatory tone seemed to make it worse. Miranda sought to rescue her by saying she reckoned it was a good idea and that maybe Jenny could come in one day to see the students' interpretations.

Toby and Jenny went to their room when the meal was finished while Anni quietly washed up and made strong coffee. They chatted in a desultory fashion over coffee and somehow it was agreed that it was pointless for Anni to go home at this time of night. She was happy to sleep on the sofa with some added cushions and a throw, would borrow toiletries from Miranda and didn't have to be at college until midday so could go home first.

When this was agreed and organised Miranda gratefully went to bed and waited for Mike.

She could hear their voices for a while and then she drifted into sleep, to be awoken by Mike sliding in beside her some time later. As he embraced her she could smell traces of French cigarette smoke and Anni's musky perfume.

Chapter 4

Anglesey

Mike had suggested that for Miranda's half-term holiday they link up with some climbing friends of his in a seaside retreat in North Wales. They travelled up in Mike's ancient Lancia which he regarded as a prized possession. The place was an old type of farmhouse with a group of converted barns and stables clustered around it. Guests stayed in the converted buildings with their own sleeping accommodation and shared cooking and eating facilities. This was to encourage a commune type of atmosphere. The place attracted creative and energetic people with busy lives who valued the opportunity to distance themselves from urban life. There was no mobile phone signal and internet access was patchy. On arrival Miranda discovered that the owner, a woman in her seventies, had been a celebrated writer and illustrator of children's books. Meeting Tania was like encountering a soulmate: she was dressed totally in black wearing harem pants, wide-sleeved tunic and even black flip flops. She had heavily kohl rimmed eyes and wore her astonishing long blonde hair swept up in a bandanna. When Miranda expressed interest in her work she showed her some of her illustrations and gave her a tour of the property which was furnished in a chaotic manner with antique furniture, vibrantly coloured cushions and fabrics. She explained that although she had been brought up in North Wales her mother was Finnish and they had made frequent trips to Finland. Her stories and pictures were inspired by the myths, legends and scenery of both Finland and North Wales.

A secluded bay with stunning views appeared down a short track below the farmhouse. Here Miranda took solitary walks early in the morning. Above the bay rose vast, ochreous stretches of limestone. A variety of bird life wheeled overhead (she learnt they were plovers, oystercatchers and curlews).

The beach was a treasure trove of shells, casts, stones and driftwood. She loved these forays to collect found items for her work. Wearing loose clothing and free of make-up, she felt uninhibited. There were rich sources here for photography, sketches and collecting.

The others were an energetic, lively and highly gregarious group; the men and some of the women were climbers and all seemed to have in-depth knowledge of the sport. In the daytime they walked along the beach, taking a route round the headland to an even more isolated bay, ate pub lunches and made forays into the nearby town (a place which seemed to have stayed rooted in the 1950s) to purchase food and drink. Evenings were spent discussing climbing, future expeditions and anecdotes of past events, sitting for hours in the large, friendly communal kitchen, fuelled by beer, wine and cider. There was much use of technical terms and debates about methods and techniques: words such as crampons, snowshoes, bivouacs, footwork, ropeless were beginning to enter into her vocabulary.

Sometimes she didn't even try to take it in but sat quietly sipping wine letting the talking become a soporific background with the same lack of responsibility to contribute as if they were talking in Mandarin.

There were constant discussions about past expeditions, achievements and problems. All of the climbers there had done some climbing on Everest and Miranda was interested in their experiences. The British Everest Expedition in 1975 when Doug Scott, Dougal Haston and Chris Bonnington climbed the North Face was an historical climb that Miranda was familiar with but she had little knowledge of current climbing practices.

'Quite honestly, Everest is now becoming a tourist destination,' one of the climbers said.
'The paths are all laid out and professional guides will take anyone who wants to pay. You could do it.'

'But surely there are dangers and accidents?' Miranda asked.

'Yeah, sure. Everest is a graveyard and a rubbish tip. It's peppered with unrecovered bodies, empty oxygen cylinders, rubbish and detritus. In fact, it's become an environmental disaster in serious need of a clean-up, but it's not like cleaning up the streets.'

Miranda's visions of the beauty of soaring snow-capped mountains were abruptly ruined. The speaker was Duncan, a guy who would be joining Mike on the Patagonia trip. He was short and stocky with curly blond hair and a weather-beaten complexion. He talked easily and pleasantly, and was less frantic and energetic in his speech than Mike. She found herself asking Duncan about the fear.

'Fear is a state of mind; you have to use it as a tool to assist you rather than let it defeat you. Instead of giving in to the fear you have to confront it and rationalise it. Climbing has to be a focused activity. You also have to have responsibility for others; you must be a team player and not just seek individual glory. Even if you get to the end of your physical adrenaline you have to help each other.'

She was to be reminded of this some time later.

'So, why do you do it?'

'Yeah, the question all non-climbers ask. Everyone is dramatically changed by reaching a summit and seeing something so much bigger than themselves.'

Naturally the conversation turned to their forthcoming expedition to the North Pillar in Patagonia.

She would miss Mike of course although she was unsure what the status of their relationship was. In some ways it was suffocating; she couldn't think of anything else when she was alone with him and when they were apart he was always in the back of her mind, leaving her with a soft thrill of excitement.

He had entered her life and taken it over in an unexpected way. He complimented her without seeming insincere; he sought her company and offered her excitement and the unexpected. He rarely asked about her work and other aspects of her life and had taken no interest in her family circumstances, accepting Toby and Jenny without question when they arrived at her flat. She supposed that he had a dedicated carpe diem attitude to life. He did talk with enthusiasm about his commitment to climbing, describing for her the intensity and the isolation.

Despite his dismissal of all things mundane and petty, he could allow irritations with life to build up until he was on a short fuse. She was mortified when he would suddenly pick fights with people in supermarket queues or shout at waiters in restaurants. These occasions were rare, but when they happened she could see a potentially uncontrollable temper.

Did she love him? No idea: she loved the experience of being with him but was unable to clearly envisage a possible future. In her mind she saw the Munch painting of 'The Kiss' and considered that the line between attraction and fear was a fine one.

Miranda wondered if she could ever live like this, away from concrete, urban noise and technology. She could certainly work here and had completed a number of promising sketches as the basis for future projects.

On the evening before their penultimate day, Mike announced he had planned a walk further afield.

'Just the two of us: I'll introduce you to some climbing, nothing strenuous, just easy stuff. We'll leave very early and catch some breakfast at a hotel near the car park before we start.' Brilliant, Miranda thought. However much she enjoyed the company of the others they were over-energetic in some ways and she wanted time alone with Mike.

There was truly some breathtakingly scenery en route. It was a steady climb. The path was sheltered between mountains and sea cliffs, and trapped the warm June sun. Miranda's artistic instincts appreciated the beauty of the rocks; limestone, quartzite and Welsh slate. After some steady walking they reached the starting point for their ascent: the view was intoxicating and she understood some of Mike's passion for the mountains. Looking at the view she felt invigorated; after the uphill walking her heart was racing and she could feel the uplifting effects of the clear air. They silently drew together and embraced. She felt almost drunk with exercise, fresh air and altitude, and wanted to stay like this, wrapped around each other.

But nothing had prepared her for so many hours of solid walking and climbing without a break. Her early morning runs, swimming and yoga practice appeared to have no impact on her fitness level and she was exhausted, hot and her walking boots were chafing uncomfortably round her ankles. Realising how tired she now was she lost the steady rhythm she had copied from Mike initially. Suddenly she slipped and twisted her foot.

She slumped on to a nearby stone while Mike checked it out.

'It's OK; maybe a minor sprain but you can cope.'

'I'm not sure if I can. I've really had enough. How much further?'

Mike looked irritated.

'You have to be joking; we're only halfway.'

'What! But you said it would be easy.'

'It is, Miranda,' he said quietly. 'So, just get up and start again.' His eyes looked cold and steely.

'I don't know if I can do much more. Can't we find a quick route to go down?'

'Even if we could I wouldn't because we are going to finish this and you need me to show you the route.'

'Please, at least let me rest for a while, and I'm hungry.'

She was aware that she was starting to whine. He delved in his rucksack and threw a Snickers bar at her.

'You can eat this while you're walking. Now get up.' And reaching down he grasped her round her wrists and hauled her roughly to her feet. The beauty of the mountain had become alienating. She felt alone: he had no sympathy and even seemed to be taking a perverse pleasure in her discomfort and dependency. Then his tone softened.

'You can do it, sweetheart. Put one foot in front of the other and don't look down.'

She climbed silently behind him, following his steady pace. At intervals he checked that she was drinking enough water and handed her a Mars bar. She felt tearful, her wrists were stinging and she was convinced that she could feel blisters and congealed blood in her boots.

Was he actually enjoying this? When they finally descended and reached the car park they drove in a tense silence to the town where they had breakfasted happily so many hours ago in The Crown and Anchor.

'We'll have a pit stop here before we drive back. Go and wash your face and clean up and I'll see you at the bar.'

With relief she washed her face, combed her hair and brushed mud off her jeans. She didn't dare examine her throbbing foot.

Mike was standing at the bar chatting to the barman, a pint of beer in front of him. Taking her round the shoulders he tilted her face up and kissed her firmly.

'That's my girl.' He led her to a corner table where he had ordered meat pies from the bar and a pot of coffee.

'This will wake you up.' They ate and drank quietly. She still felt nervous with him and didn't know what to say. He really did seem to be oblivious to her pain and tiredness.

Back in their room at the barn he helped her in from the car and instructed her to get undressed and lie on the bed while he ran a bath. The bathroom was a particularly splendid feature of their accommodation, with a claw-footed bath under a corner window with a deep sill. He had filled the bath with hot-scented water and had lit candles on the window sill. She sank into it and at last felt safe. Despite the pain and feeling disturbed by Mike's attitude she had to acknowledge a sneaking sense of latent excitement and pride in her achievement. So this is what climbing was all about: beauty, pain and terror, and then the urge to do it again?

'By the way,' Mike said, 'as it's our last night, Tania has invited the whole group to have dinner with her and her husband. She likes you; don't think she'd have asked us otherwise.'

Her first thought was, 'Oh God, I'm so, so tired and the prospect of a social evening loomed like an endurance test.' But maybe it was preferable to spending it alone with Mike after the tensions of the day, and she did love Tania's company. When she returned to the bedroom Mike was waiting with arnica for the bruised foot and a crepe bandage for her now very swollen ankle.

'I suggest you take a couple of paracetamols and then you'll feel great.'

Tania and her husband were waiting for them in their farmhouse all-purpose living area which was fitted with restored pine. An actual church pew stood by one wall and French windows at the back of the room overlooked a stone flagged patio and sloping garden.

Tania was elaborately dressed in her accustomed black, enhanced by some glittering jet jewellery. She had prepared a meal with local produce: Welsh lamb, market vegetables, home-baked bread and local goat's cheese. An endless supply of red wine was poured. There were much laughter and expressions of pleasure at how much the group had enjoyed themselves. Tania's husband engaged the men in climbing talk for a while and then diverse conversations sprang up around the table. Tania sat next to Miranda and explained how she gained inspiration from the myths and legends of the area to inform her stories and drawings.

After coffee and a glass of flamed Sambuca, and with the influence of wine and pain killers, Miranda felt on another plane. She was in a dream-like state. She had forgiven Mike for his cruelty on the walk and was now more than ready to return with him to their room, where she felt that their lovemaking was the best ever.

She succeeded in getting to the beach the next morning, despite a hangover feeling and a very sore foot and ankle. As she gazed out to sea, watching the birds and feeling invigorated already, she considered how like a dream this break had been, and the unpleasant episode with Mike had diminished in significance.

As they were leaving Tania came out to wish them goodbye.

'It was interesting talking to you, Miranda. Good luck with your exhibition,' and then, quietly inclining her head in Mike's direction, she said.

'You've got a charmer there but there's more than a hint of danger, so take care.'

It was an unsettling remark. Tania was a thoughtful, perceptive woman and Miranda had valued her opinions, but this advice was as unexpected as it was unwanted. Miranda admired the energy and vigour of the older woman, her self-contained confidence and refusal to adhere to convention. She was sad to read several months later in an obituary column that Tania had died.

Late Sunday afternoon in June was not the best time to arrive back in Camden Town.

Traffic clogged the streets, the air was heavy with diesel fumes and, after the cleanliness and wide seascapes of Anglesey, the town looked flat and prosaic. Already Miranda's thoughts had turned to the next day and the start of half-term. Faculty meetings with Malcolm and Angela, sorting out groups of students who would be returning to study next year and helping with the show of work to be displayed at the Design Centre in Islington. Mike dropped her off at her flat and carried her stuff upstairs, being very solicitous about her sprained ankle.

'Look, I know you're tired, but why don't we go out later for a quiet pizza and glass of wine. It'll help you to make the transition and, anyway, I'd like a bit more time with you before you start your manic working again.'

She decided this was a good idea and it made her less resentful when she found Toby and Jenny sprawled around her living room with some people they had met at a bar. And, she was convinced that she could smell weed. How ironic if they managed to get her evicted from the flat. She took Toby to task about this in the kitchen but he was unrepentant.

'For God's sake M, we've been here before. Have you forgotten what you were like as a student? You did all of this stuff.'

'Maybe I did but as I keep reminding you, I work now, I have a career, and this is my flat that I pay for that you're staying in for free. So, how about a few ground rules? Check before you fill the place with friends and no more weed. And stay out of the way of Julian.'

'OK, will do. And anyway, I've got a job now.'
'Great: where?'

'Well, it's sort of a job. I met some guys who have a recording studio in Soho and they offered me the chance to write reviews of gigs for them. I showed them one I'd done already and they were impressed. I'm not actually on the payroll but they'll pay me for each review and then maybe I can get involved in the technology side of things. Oh, and of course I get free tickets for the gigs. I'll keep on my bar job at nights; I really do want to get sorted M, to prepare for the baby.'

And Miranda could hear the wistfulness in his tone: her baby brother taking responsibility for his own baby. If only it worked out.

Chapter 5

The Yoga Room

Monday morning at 7.30 am and Miranda was in the yoga room. The yoga room had been set up by a guy called Vikram, who lived in a rather decaying property the wrong side of King's Cross on the Farringdon Road. He was an experienced yoga practitioner who dedicated a spacious room for yoga practice and invited people to share it with him. It was not an organised class but an opportunity to practise individually and silently in a room with others. Miranda had discovered him via an advert in an organic shop and cafe on Marchmont Street that she sometimes frequented, and instantly she was drawn to the idea. If she caught an early tube to King's Cross she could fit in an hour before college. Vikram acknowledged her as she went in and found a corner of the room to practise in. She had developed her own routine and it was so much easier to carry out this silent regimen with other people around. In fact, it was almost like being in church. The yoga poses were soothing and meditational, allowing her to move out of her surroundings into an inner world. After one of these sessions she could approach the college day in a relatively relaxed state.

The College

At college the culmination of the foundation course year was the public exhibition of their work at the Islington Design Centre. After this, some students returned to take other courses while others found places in higher education or sought employment.

Tutors were involved in all aspects of the work. Miranda had responsibility for her own student group and would be expected to share the rota for the exhibition with the other full-time members of the department. Late Monday afternoon she was sorting materials in her room and contemplating when she could fit in work on her MA studies now that formal classes for her had finished. She was interrupted by Jude, her face glowing with rage.

'God, she's a cow.'

'Who?'

'Who do you think? Angela. Telling me off in that Madam smarty-pants way of hers.

"This college doesn't revolve around you, Jude. You can't just choose to go your own way. There are other students here and we do have procedures to follow; if you're not prepared to adhere to them it may be necessary to ask you to leave." Adhere? What kind of a word is that?'

'OK, calm down Jude. Do you want me to have a word with Angela to try and sort it out?'

'No, I'll sort it myself. Anyway, she's given me a "friendly warning", whatever the hell that is, but next time she says it'll be a formal warning. I thought this was meant to be a fucking art college, not a prison, for God's sake. I came here because I expected freedom. Choosing and going my own way is exactly what I want to do.'

Privately Miranda thought that art and creativity weren't just about freedom; discipline and commitment were also essential factors. However, she did share Jude's feelings about Angela. There were very few members of staff who had not been alienated by this brother and sister team. They exerted control over the faculty like Renaissance despots, issuing instructions and checking on every movement, yet showing little interest in becoming involved in hands-on work and regular contact with the students except for the occasional unannounced entry into the teaching rooms as if hoping to catch the tutors out in some misdemeanour or deviation from their plan. Faculty meetings, targets and finance were the topics that interested them. They were unwelcome in the staff social areas and were nicknamed Morticia and the Prince of Darkness.

To get her off the topic Miranda asked Jude about her artistic aspirations and Jude showed her some sketches of clothes that she was working on, fashion design being her ultimate objective. They chatted for a while about the contemporary designers that she admired and Miranda suggested some areas for her to follow-up. By the time Jude left she had calmed down and Miranda returned to the task of tidying her room.

Various students and staff had been in and out of her room during the afternoon and when Jude left at last it was quiet. She was kneeling on the floor sorting out books and files when she heard the door click open and close.

Joel was leaning against it. She flushed and felt embarrassed and then angry with herself.

'For God's sake,' she thought, 'he's the one who was out of line. I should be shouting at him, not looking away like a silly teenager.' It occurred to her that she had never really looked at Joel properly and it was only now that she saw how tall he was. His thinness made him look slight but he must be nearly six foot with lanky dark hair and a pale complexion. She noticed there were traces of acne around his mouth. Despite his thin frame she realised that he could be strong.

He took his time before he spoke and then said.

'I left some of my stuff here. Is it OK to look for it?'

She had to say something to him. If she had really decided not to refer to the assault again then she would have to behave normally.

'Yes, go ahead,' and then, 'what are you thinking of doing next term Joel? I noticed that you haven't enrolled for any courses here.'

'No, think I've had enough of this and I need to get a paid job, you know, my Mum ...' and his voice tailed off.

'Yeah, sure, what are you looking for?' (While wondering who would want to employ someone as taciturn as Joel.)

'Maybe in a graphic design studio, you know, that sort of thing.'

'Well, best of luck.'

He spent what seemed an unnecessary amount of time sorting through things the students had left and then came up to her desk.

'Did you find my drawing? I left it on your table.'

Miranda remembered the pencil sketch which she had thrust into the back of a drawer. Her anger returned with this confirmation that he had deliberately left it there.

'Actually, I did. And what was meant to be the purpose of it?'

'But didn't you like it? I felt it was a pretty good resemblance.'

'It might have been but I wasn't aware that I had marks and scratches over my neck and shoulders.'

'Yeah, well, it's an interpretation. It's not a photograph.'

There was nothing she wanted to say to him. When he had gone she found herself going over all the unpleasant episodes and events that she now associated with Joel, and again she tried to understand his motivation. Did he imagine that she liked him and worse, welcomed these attentions? Many of the male students did adopt a playfully flirtatious relationship with their more engaging female tutors. It was harmless fun and Miranda was happy to go along with it. It reminded her of her own youthful days and made her feel included in their lives. Some of the young men she would have been attracted to if she was still their age. But the one she had certainly never thought of in this way was Joel. In fact, she admitted to herself that she found him quite repulsive.

But he was leaving college and therefore, presumably, would be out of her life.

How wrong she was to be.

The British Library

Miranda was in the British Library working on her MA study. 'Munch and Hammershoi: Their Nordic Ghosts' was a subtitle to her thesis which considered the influence of environmental factors on the paintings of these two artists.

What was it about the two artists that made them so melancholy and mysterious? Their interior scenes were quiet and haunting and thinly populated. Hammershoi's city scenes and Munch's landscapes were frequently devoid of human presence. When they featured figures, the subjects avoided the gaze of the viewer; as if there was something to hide, ashamed even. The colours that Hammershoi used were often subdued but by no means monochromatic; instead, they used delicate shifting palettes and clever use of light. She thought of him when he had visited Britain, in his apartment opposite the British Museum, painting the city streets at quiet times of day; and Munch with his lodgings overlooking the Seine, painting views of the river: both so close to human activity, but never seeming to be part of it.

She had on the desk in front of her copies of Munch's paintings from his Frieze of Life sequence.

He had been controversial and had provoked outrage with his evocations of death, illness and tormented souls. It was a pity that the one work of his that commanded instant recognition was one that had been commercially trashed and reproduced everywhere, even being reduced to a sign for a pub chain. She studied his painting entitled 'Ashes', noting his technique of using wax crayon and tempera. It was both brave and sensual. The painting focused on a female figure; long, unbrushed red hair cascaded over her shoulders and the white fabric dress she was wearing was ripped down the front, exposing a red camisole. Was it a violation? Had she been attacked? The clue might have been the male figure at the edge of the painting bent over with his head in his hands. This could have suggested remorse yet it didn't seem that way to Miranda. The woman held a dominant position and it was as though she was the victor. Was this possibly a more subtle form of his vampire paintings? The background to the picture was a thickly wooded forest and stones. She admired the potency of the rhythm and colour but found it had an unpleasant effect on her mood.

For Miranda it was the sequence of the 'Vampire/Kiss' paintings that attracted her, exploiting as they did the links between love and suffering, pain and sexuality. More uplifting were his mood-filled landscapes, painted in summer months spent on Norwegian islands. It was interesting that both Munch and Hammershoi had links with the dramatists Ibsen and Strindberg. There was a quality that was intrinsically theatrical in their interior scenes. She turned her attention to look at how Munch's work had developed into his Green Room series with garishly coloured brothel interiors. She read again the text he had written to accompany the sequence.

'Far away his eye fell upon a couple. A red-headed woman and a man walking along pressed close together. A shock passed through him, the blood rushed in his ears and the dreadful suspicion was there again.'

But the painting she kept returning to was 'The Vampire', sometimes called 'The Kiss'. This was the one that most intrigued her and she had shared this fascination with her students. She remembered how they had discussed the possible implications and the motives of the painter. Some of the students saw it as sinister or macabre: Jacob had suggested that it could be a positive scene with the man seeking comfort from the woman and being consoled by her, but Francesca was convinced that the position of the woman leaning over the man's neck implied that he was her prey.

They did all agree that the painting had a disturbing atmosphere and that they wanted to ask questions about the situation and the narrative behind it. They had used words like sorrow, anger, betrayal and passion, and looked for clues in the painting, like the fact that there was so much black in the work. Miranda's own interpretation was that the painting managed to convey both sadness and beauty, and she was impressed by the sensuality of the scene. Munch's original title had been 'Love and Pain', and there were days like today when Miranda felt these words encompassed the contradictions in her life.

A man working near her in the reading room dropped a book; the reverberation brought her back to the present and her immediate surroundings. She had worked there most of the day, lulled by the soft swishing library sounds and clicking on and off of reading lights. She had emerged occasionally for coffee and water and, not wanting to break the spell of her working rhythm, had chosen not to leave the building at lunchtime but to go across the mezzanine floor to the balcony cafe where she ate a pastry scone and drank more coffee.

Now she was slightly giddy from concentrated study, plus the paracetamols that she had been taking to cope with her still-throbbing foot and ankle. The effects of the injury were lingering for longer than she had expected and made walking difficult when it flared up. After his initial consideration when they had returned to their room following the climbing incident, Mike had ceased to be interested in her injury. He had the super-fit person's contempt for disability and illness. Frequently now, he seemed irritated with her when she couldn't walk far. When they were out with friends he would walk ahead of her in animated chat, apparently forgetting she was there.

Now this Munch quotation had stirred suspicion in her heart again. The hair might be a different colour, but she thought again of Anni standing closely with Mike on many occasions, sitting cosily with him in her flat and walking with him down the street when all three were going to the wine bar while Miranda lagged behind.

Enough: she needed to get out.

The heat hit her as she emerged on to the huge paved courtyard. Susannah had been working at college and they had arranged to meet when Miranda was free. A text message confirmed that she was waiting for her in Russell Square Gardens. Once she had negotiated the toxic horror of the Euston Road her route took her along Marchmont Street, past the university halls of residence, now occupied by overseas students on summer courses The Greasy Spoon Cafe which provided cheap meals for penniless students and hungry workmen, the second-hand and gay and lesbian bookstores, and the vegan cafe. The architecture of the flats surrounding the Brunswick Centre made her feel that she was approaching a liner out at sea.

As she rounded the corner towards Russell Square Station a voice shouted.

'Hi, Miranda!'

Some of her students were sitting at the metal tables outside Pret A Manger. The twins, Jessica and Francesca were there, a quiet friendly girl called Ruth whom Miranda liked very much and, surprisingly, Joel. She wasn't aware that he was part of their crowd, or of any crowd come to that, but as he lived relatively near maybe he had met them accidentally. She sat down briefly to chat with them about their plans for holidays, courses for next year and part-time work. Joel sat listening, his eyes drifting towards Miranda, but making no attempt to contribute.

A buzzing noise announced the arrival of Francesca's Italian boyfriend on a silver Vespa. Miranda was reminded of the young people she used to observe in Italian towns, lounging around cafe tables smoking and talking, and ever ready to leap on scooters and tear off around the streets with much panache amid resounding shouts of ciao.

The arrival of the boyfriend interrupted the conversation and Miranda took the opportunity to continue to the gardens.

The gardens in Russell Square were a magnet to Londoners and visitors alike, a haven of flowers, foliage and overarching plane trees in this noisy, traffic-clogged area. People were sprawled on the grass reading or sleeping, groups of Italian students on school trips sat in circles with backpacks distributed around them, children and birds splashed in the fountain and a regular stream of people used the paths as throughways. Susannah was sitting at a cafe table with her two daughters who had been brought in after school to meet her by the current au pair.

'Hi Miranda, you look like you could do with a soothing cold drink. I've just tempted these two with the best Italian ice cream in London (after Marine Ices, of course). Fancy some?'

'No, I'll stick with the drink, thanks.'

Susannah was chatting to the Czech au pair about some arrangements for the evening.

Miranda sipped her cool Peroni, closed her eyes in the warm sunlight and listened to the cries of children and the frantic barking of dogs chasing squirrels up the trees.

'Hey, this is the life,' Susannah said. 'Beer at 4.00 in the afternoon and it's Saturday tomorrow.'

Miranda opened her eyes to agree with her and, looking to her right where two dogs were squabbling for rights over a squirrel that was never going to be their prize, she saw Joel quietly walking along the path to the other side of the gardens. Her mood of peaceful meditation was broken.

However hard she tried to avoid it, the problem of Joel was constantly lurking at the back of her mind.

He was probably the only one of her students who did not respond to her and with whom she had had no real contact, until of course the horror of the assault.

During sessions in the teaching room he continued to be self-absorbed and distant from the others. In the past she had barely noticed him around college but now, looking back, she realised that he had usually been alone. To her he had been nondescript and, she had to admit, very unappealing. He lacked the physical attraction, charm or the engaging personality of the majority of her students. If she had thought about him at all she would have pitied him, but now he had forced himself into her life and had made her think about him in a different way. What was it that he wanted? The physical contact, although sickening, could have been explained away as an impetuous adolescent act but the other episodes, where she was convinced he was following her, had more sinister implications. Was he actually attracted to her and did he expect her to respond? She couldn't begin to imagine what was going on in his head but the one certainty was that she now had reason to fear him.

Chapter 6

Camden Town

The private view in Kate and Paul's studio was scheduled for the Saturday after the end of term, which coincided with Miranda's birthday. To Miranda this was a big opportunity, to have her work on public display in a tasteful gallery in the context of the work of the studio group. After all the hours spent in the studio with paint splattered clothes and wearing old jeans and fingerless mittens to ward off the cold, she was ready to look and feel good.

In a small boutique store in Camden Town she found a dress in soft grey silk, sleeveless and with a gently ruched knee-length skirt and cowl-shaped hood which swept over the shoulders: a simple, but very effective garment, which she added sparkle to with high-heeled silver sandals. She had noticed the dress on a window shopping wander with Anni. Over ice creams in Marine Ices afterwards, Anni, who had been invited to the private view, had mentioned that she was unsure what to wear as her wardrobe was limited and she hadn't been able to afford anything new for some time. Miranda casually considered whether she might have something to lend her.

As they left the ice cream parlour they turned down an alleyway of second-hand book and jewellery stores. One particular store always intrigued Miranda. It was a store owned by practising Jews which closed on Saturdays and sold mainly religious artefacts but also held a collection of second-hand jewellery. Rings, bracelets and watches predominated. Miranda would look at these and try to imagine the stories behind the people who had felt it necessary to part with them. Of special appeal was an ancient silver choker with a black scarab pendant. It was a fascinating item which she felt certain would have an interesting history.

On the Thursday evening after college Miranda went straight to the studio to put the final touches to her triptych. Rebecca greeted her with fresh coffee as always and had even thoughtfully left out a cheese baguette for her to eat while she worked. Some of the others were there; Max was arranging the safe removal of his bronze sculpture of a bird of prey which was scarily realistic. Rebecca's husband, Simon, had arranged to transport all the work to the gallery later that evening when the roads were quiet and the shops closed. Arrangements for the hanging were being made by Kate and Paul, and some local caterers were providing drinks and canapés.

She was quickly absorbed in her work, checking varnish on the painting and the mounts on her sketches. When the final sketch was mounted and she was satisfied with her main canvas of the triptych she collected her things, realising that apart from Rebecca and Simon she was the last to leave. It was still warm as she left the studio via the garden, which was attractively wild and reminded her of semi-neglected, nineteenth-century Italianate gardens. There was a strong aroma of honeysuckle in the night air. The windows of the studio had misted over because even in summer it was necessary to use the oil heater in the evenings. The shadow of a figure seemed to pass over the window near the door but Miranda was uncertain.

Why would anyone be in the garden at the side of the shed? As she walked awkwardly, burdened by her college bag and her portfolio, she saw someone leaving the garden by the side gate. She had a feeling that it was Joel.

Feeling slightly queasy at the realisation that he may have been following her; Miranda made for the security of her flat. So, the problem wasn't resolved. She had assumed that once term ended she would see no more of Joel. There would, of course, be an opportunity for the students to return to college in August to discuss their results, and a number of them would stay on for further courses. The majority would either have secured places at universities or Art Schools or would be job-hunting. It had seemed to her unlikely that Joel with his disaffected attitude would be sufficiently interested to follow another course of study, although in fact it occurred to her that she had never considered what he might want to do until their brief conversation in her room. He had impinged on her consciousness so little until he had recently made his presence felt.

She was met by the sound of laughter as she ascended the stairs to the flat and was taken aback to find Mike and Anni with Toby and Jenny sprawled around the living room. All seemed to be on the verge of tipsy and were enjoying a shared joke.

'Hi, am I missing something here?' She asked, feeling the annoyance of the sober person when everyone else is humorously merry.

'Sorry, love. Mike got up to hug her. I ran into Anni earlier when she was out looking for a dress to wear for your view so she asked my advice.'

'Yeah, he was really helpful. I found something in a vintage shop that I could afford. I'll show you.'

Anni rushed off to Miranda's bedroom and returned wearing a long heavy cotton, dull cream dress with some lace stitching around the scooped neckline. Trust Anni to find a strange old garment that she looked really good in.

'It's great, but what's all laughter in aid of?' Miranda knew she sounded petulant and childish but she did feel left out of this cosy foursome.

'We just suddenly felt like some bubbly so we shared a bottle of Prosecco,' Mike said. 'There's probably some left for you.'

Hardly able to conceal her irritation, Miranda accepted the glass that Toby poured for her and pleading exhaustion, said that she would see them all the next evening and went off to bed. So, Mike had 'just happened' to meet Anni and they felt it would be a good idea to share fizzy wine and giggle like schoolkids while she was working seriously to plan for her important private view.

After a tormented few hours of dreams where Miranda envisaged Munch's 'The Vampire', but instead of Munch's protagonists it was Anni and Mike as the subjects with Anni's tresses cascading over Mike's sturdy shoulders she woke, shuddering, in a cold sweat and then finally fell into a sound sleep, waking to a feeling of renewed energy. Once outside to begin her run she felt that she had got things back into perspective and used the running time to plan her day as a prelude to the view. She felt suddenly uninhibited and in the mood for a new experience. Something she had contemplated for a while was getting a tattoo but it had always seemed too frivolous. But now she felt like taking the risk.

She spent the morning in a hectic cleaning and sorting of the flat while Toby and Jenny were out somewhere and arranged an appointment at a tattoo parlour for the afternoon.

After some reflection the design she chose was a tiny serpent to be tattooed on her upper left arm. This would leave it visible for evening and summer wear but allow for concealment if it ever seemed inappropriate. Feeling risky and happy with her decision she answered a call from Rebecca who said she wanted to celebrate their first gallery showing as a group and had booked a table for them to eat after at a French place with long wooden tables and an eclectic menu. All studio participants and partners were invited.

She was due at the gallery at 6.30 and by 6.00 she was ready. A noise of doors opening and footsteps on the stairs announced the arrival of Mike with Anni. Surprised, as she hadn't expected to see them until the private view, she was delighted with Mike's reaction to her appearance and his lingering kiss.

'I wanted to see you before this evening to give you your birthday present. Well, we both wanted to give it to you. It's meant to be a surprise.'

It certainly was. She unwrapped the slim flat package and found herself looking at a delicate life drawing of … Mike. It was beautifully executed and carried with it hints of sensuality.

Miranda's artistic training had accustomed her to looking at portraits and life drawings from the point of view of the relationship between the artist and sitter, and what did this imply? Hours of intimate and private time together, while Mike sat for Anni.

There was an uncomfortable silence broken by Mike.

'Well, what do you think?' he said.

She realised they were both waiting for a reaction and their faces looked so blameless and innocent. The professional in her took over and she was able to lavish praise on the quality of Anni's work but couldn't help herself from saying.

'But, how did you manage to keep this is secret from me?' Mike smoothly supplied the answer.

'All of those evenings when you were at the studio. In fact, the night you came home and sounded off at us when we'd been drinking Prosecco was the evening Anni had finished it.'

She was being stupid. It was an excellent drawing and Anni, who was unable to afford much in the way of presents, had used the resources she did have, her talent and her time, to create something that was genuinely personal for Miranda. And didn't this put a positive spin on her relationship with Mike, if he wanted her to have this permanent memento?

None of these rational thoughts however, could stop the nervously palpitating feeling in her insides.

She needed to get out and focus on the evening ahead.

The Gallery

The paintings looked good on the clear, minimalist white/grey walls of the gallery, a fairly narrow space with a spiral staircase twisting up to a mezzanine floor. By the window at the front of the gallery a table had been set out with wine and canapés, and a large vase of carefully arranged mixed white flowers. An enormous wax candle stood on a metal stand near the table, its glow casting an almost ethereal light over the room. Now that she was here and feeling good about her appearance, Miranda could allow herself to relax, talk to the others and praise their work.

Suddenly Kate was at her side, wanting to introduce her to a couple who were interested in her triptych.

'They're interior designers and are refurbishing their own apartment in Maida Vale. Come and meet them.'

Miriam and Adrian Sorensen were on the mezzanine floor absorbing the details of her triptych. 'Interior designers' sounded somewhat awesome but they were a friendly, engaging Jewish couple in their early fifties with a keen interest in collecting contemporary art. Miriam was particularly warm and enthusiastic.

'We really like the concept of your triptych. It would look excellent in our living area. So – we'd like to purchase it.'

A deep pink flush suffused Miranda's cheeks. She had longed for and imagined this moment. She had dared to hope that her smaller paintings might have attracted buyers but hadn't expected this sale. Paul joined them and brought glasses of wine to celebrate. Fortunately for Miranda he took control of the conversation, exploring the features of Miranda's work and congratulating the Sorensens on their choice. Her feeling of naive embarrassment was replaced by a tingling euphoria. Other members of the studio group appeared and, wine glass in hand,

Miranda withdrew from the people standing around her painting and tried to stand back and see it with their eyes. As she leaned on the spiral staircase her gaze fell on the people wandering around the lower floor. She noticed Jasmin looking totally exotic in a flame-coloured sari with gold threads and Jamal in protective role as usual. She reflected that in some ways it must be very reassuring to be so cared for. Then, near the door and away from the chattering clusters, she was aware of Mike and Anni. Anni was leaning back against the wall, looking slightly flushed and happy with a glass in her hand and Mike was facing her with one arm propped on the wall above her head in a way that could easily signify casual friendship, but which Miranda interpreted as an intimate gesture. A pang of anxiety went through Miranda and, she had to admit, jealousy. Why was Anni so close with Mike? At the start of their friendship Miranda had welcomed her as a warm friend and someone she could confide in and share details of her life. Anni had always been agreeable, complimenting Miranda on her work, admiring her relationship with her students and willing to fall in with any social arrangements that Miranda suggested.

But Miranda was becoming increasingly aware that Anni was quietly insinuating herself into her life. There was a seductive quality to her friendship; she was gregarious, a good conversationalist and was apparently interested in every aspect of Miranda's life. She encouraged confidences, listened and sympathised. Yet, on reflection, Miranda considered there was something vicarious about Anni's involvement.

Her role had been a passive one, accepting all invitations but rarely suggesting anything herself, making herself very agreeable to Miranda's friends and studio acquaintances, and offering to accompany Miranda on shopping trips, etc. Anni was often in Miranda's flat, staying the night if it got late. Miranda, who was naturally generous, had allowed Anni to borrow her clothes and jewellery, and was willing to buy an extra round on the many occasions when Anni was short of cash. She had become integrated into Miranda's social circle, knew her way around Miranda's flat in a familiar manner, had worn her clothes and her perfume, and had promptly made friends with Toby and Jenny. Did she also want Mike? Miranda could now see how this could happen and could even imagine how Anni might justify it. Having been badly hurt by her own failed marriage she probably regarded the love game as just that; a game to be played and won if you could.

Once she began to think about it, Miranda found herself accumulating the evidence: the number of occasions when Anni and Mike had 'just happened' to meet each other in Camden Town, the occasions when she had worked late in the studio after college and returned to find them ensconced in her flat, occasionally watching TV but more often chatting quietly over a bottle of wine. How did they both manage to be there at the same time? OK, Mike had a key and Jenny was often there now to answer the door, but it did seem to be ultra-convenient. Mike had gone with Anni when she bought her vintage dress for this evening and they had secretly collaborated on the life sketches as her present, spending time alone together so that Mike could sit for Anni. She considered the less than subtle hints passed by Susannah and other friends when they casually mentioned seeing Anni and Mike out together. When she questioned him about these meetings he came up with plausible explanations: they were buying food for

Miranda because she was working so hard, one of them wanted advice from the other about something, Anni had asked Mike to accompany her to the solicitor's because she felt upset to go alone. And so it went on. And then, horrifically, her dream came back to her: that haunting image of Mike and Anni in Munch's painting.

Is that what Anni was? A metaphorical vampire; feeding off Miranda and a life that she wanted for herself? My God, she was being ridiculous. She had to get a grip.

When she arrived downstairs to tell them of her successful sale they were both genuinely delighted.

'Why you should be surprised I don't know,' Anni said. 'You have undoubted talent.'

Mike added, '

Just imagine M, your painting on display in some up-market apartment. Think of the people who will see it and the possibilities of further work.'

The Sorensons confirmed details of the sale and arrangements to collect the painting, taking Miranda's personal details so that they could invite her to visit them and see the painting in situ.

Later, in the French brasserie that Rebecca had booked for the post-view party, Miranda spent some time with Kate and Paul going over the possibility of more work for the gallery. She was interested in producing a series of paintings on small canvases depicting scenes and images that she had stored in her imagination. She had thought of naming the series 'Contemporary Icons'. Her plan was to use the images she sourced from her observation of historical buildings, church architecture and locations that had a particular appeal for her. Her sketches and artefacts collected in Anglesey would furnish her with seascape images and she wanted to investigate baroque architecture during the Portuguese city holiday that she had planned for the end of August with Mike.

Kate and Paul responded well to her proposal, offering to give her the back wall of the studio to display the pictures in the autumn to see how well they would sell. They liked the idea of affordable items that could be bought individually as presents or collected by anyone who was more enthusiastic. A series of forty was decided on and they would provide facilities for reproducing any that were popular.

Flushed with excitement both at the sale of her triptych and the prospect of this exciting commission Miranda looked around the table at her fellow artists and their partners. Giddy with champagne and lack of food she was taken aback when Max stood up and proposed a birthday toast to Miranda.

He congratulated Miranda on her successful sale as he kissed her warmly and said,
'How I've wanted an excuse to do that. You know that I've always fancied you, Tush.'

When Rebecca had extended the invitation to the partners of the studio crowd she had in passing said,
'Oh, Miranda, do please invite Anni. She has been so interested in our work and I think she'd enjoy it.'

An invitation to Anni to join them for the meal was not something Miranda wanted or had anticipated but it was impossible to ignore the request, so Anni had been duly invited and was, of course, sitting at the other end of the table with Mike. As she looked at them Mike looked up and their eyes met. He mimed that she should join them and when she did said,

'I hope our brilliant artist can drag herself away from her admirers.'

Anni excused herself to go outside for a cigarette and then Mike drew Miranda close to him and handed her a small parcel.

'Happy birthday, my clever girl.'

Wrapped in velvety red tissue paper was the silver scarab choker.

Chapter 7

Camden Town

On a sultry afternoon in Camden Town, Miranda sat by the open window of her living room working on her icon project. She had moved her worktable under the window and had spread out her sketch books and reference material while she plotted the designs.

She was planning three areas to explore: architectural inspired shapes and images (some from scenes she had caught on photographs), angles of interesting buildings and urban spaces, seascapes based on her drawings and collections from Anglesey featuring rocks, shells, stones and driftwood, and the third section would consist of images that for her had resonances, like wine goblets, a tiled wall, a piece of jewellery.

Some of these she intended to research in more detail in Lisbon because, although it was a Western European city, in many ways it was still in the past and possessed a wealth of unspoilt cultural heritage. Initial designs for the seascapes she began working on now, using a variety of mixed media to convey moods influenced by light, textures and colour. For the large stones she was building up images using dampened brown and cream paper, adding detail with charcoal and graphite. For others she would aim to recapture colour, the intense blue of the sea and the shades and depth of the limestone crags.

Thinking of the planned visit to Lisbon she looked for her diary to check the departure dates. It wasn't on her work table so she concluded that she must have left it in college (unusual, as she was so meticulous about carrying it about with her). It was a Taschen diary dedicated to Munch which featured an illustration on each page. The diary had obvious uses like recording appointments and key dates and she also used it to jot down ideas for lessons, details of books and films that she would like to buy or see and useful addresses and contacts. In fact, it was an invaluable source of reminders that she really didn't want to lose.

A slight breeze through the window stirred the leaves on the tree on the pavement; how she could do with that bracing sea breeze of Anglesey at this moment. The street was noisy today; she could hear children's voices and loud music coming from a nearby building, and two people on the street seemed to be having a violent argument in a language she didn't recognise.

It was because of the noise that she didn't hear footsteps on the stairs until Toby burst in.

'Hi, just seen a weird guy kind of hanging round outside. Seemed to be looking at all the bells. Asked him what he wanted and he was pretty vague. Then he asked did Miranda Martin live here.'

Miranda had a queasy feeling inside.

'And did you tell him?'

'Sort of; at least I said "why?" and he mumbled something and walked off. Bit of a pillock I reckon. Does he sound like anyone you know?'

'Not sure.'

But she knew alright. So, now Joel had established that she lived here. What would his next move be?

Keen to change the subject she said.

'Haven't seen much of Jenny today. Seems to spend a long time in your room.'

'Yeah, actually, getting a bit worried about her; she's spending so much time sleeping and lounging around in there now her exams are finished. Can't be good for the baby. I'll try to get her to have a walk with me before I go to work at Weatherspoons this evening.'

Amazing; Toby the doting father to be, encouraging Jenny to eat healthily, going to medical appointments with her and showing real concern. Miranda felt a pang that her younger brother was preparing to face so much responsibility. In fact she shared his concerns about Jenny. Her life revolved around Toby and their relationship, and now that he was working at variable times she spent much time alone in the flat, giving little indication of what she was doing.

Jenny was very slender with dark hair which accentuated the ethereal paleness of her face. Her quietness and aura of lassitude reminded Miranda of a figure in a religious painting. Her apparent delicacy and passivity was no doubt due at least in part to her overbearing mother who seemed to have planned Jenny's life from the moment of conception to her education and, no doubt, her marriage. Miranda could well understand Toby's attraction for the girl physically (she was undeniably pretty and seemed vulnerable) but what on earth did they talk about? Virtually every attempt at conversation with Jenny ended in a cul-de-sac, with her answering in either monosyllable, nodding agreement or just looking vague and uninterested. Being in a room alone with her usually involved an embarrassing silence and a desperate searching for suitable topics that might engage her.

Since Jenny and Toby had been living in her flat, Miranda had become aware of Jenny's strange eating habits. She rarely seemed to eat much, apart from bowls of muesli with skimmed milk which she prepared most mornings and then ate at various stages throughout the day, usually while wandering around the flat. The bowls would then be left muesli-encrusted in various inappropriate places. They had arranged initially that Miranda would let them use her supplies of non-food staples, with Toby and Jenny taking their turn to replace items, and Miranda had also offered access to any basic items in the cupboard, but the agreement was that they should buy all their own food. But, as with most flat sharing arrangements, Miranda frequently found that milk, bread, cheese and jars of jam and peanut butter had been used up because they had 'forgotten to buy anything'.

This was irritating but what was more concerning was that the small freezer which was kept on top of the fridge had been opened and chunks of frozen bread had been broken off. Jars of preserves were left with their lids off and teaspoons jammed inside. Miranda could only assume that Jenny was responsible but found it too difficult to accuse her. The teaspoons in jars looked like a binge or a lazy, careless way of eating but the frozen bread was more problematic.

One Friday evening Miranda had called in at a local patisserie to buy a tarte tatin and some individual almond tarts and cheesecakes. Her intention was to invite a few friends for coffee and cake after some drinks in the wine bar. As they gathered in her living room Miranda made coffee in her stove-top Moka and opened the fridge for the pastries. Curiously, the tarte tatin had a hole in the centre and a scoop removed, apparently by a finger, and several of the individual tartlets had been nibbled. With frustration she carefully repaired the damage by cutting all the cakes into small pieces. As she was clearing up after the guests had left, Jenny wandered in.

'Ok if I watch telly. Can't seem to sleep?'

'Hardly surprising,' Miranda thought, as she seemed to sleep half the day, but now had to be the time to confront her.

'Yeah, sure.'

Then, as an apparent afterthought,

'Jenny, you're welcome to share if I buy some cakes but if you'd wanted some why didn't you just cut yourself a slice instead of tasting; it kind of messed up their appearance.'

The look that Jenny gave her was uncharacteristically bold.

'I don't know what you're talking about.'

'I mean the cakes in the fridge, Jenny. Thought maybe you'd had some pieces out of them.'

'Why would I want to do that?'

'Quite; but who else would have?' Miranda thought.

'I don't eat cake: I'm on a diet.'

The next morning when Miranda returned from her Saturday run Jenny was sitting at the table in the living room, reading and eating a breakfast of coffee and a plate of left over tarte tatin.

After that episode Miranda often returned in the day to find Jenny slumped in the living room watching TV or sitting on the tiny fire escape balcony from the kitchen contemplating the back garden area. On Miranda's entrance she would acknowledge her and then disappear to the spare room to listen to music.

Although she had resented the loss of her privacy when Toby and Jenny had first arrived, she welcomed their presence now at times when she felt anxious about Joel's attempts to intrude in her life.

When the temperature had dropped a bit she took a walk and stopped off at a supermarket to buy groceries. Later she prepared a cool salad of leaves, feta cheese, olives and flat bread, and poured herself a large glass of chilled wine as a reward for her afternoon's work.

Jenny wandered in, looking more awake than she often did and rather virtuously said.

'I'm going to make myself some herbal tea; can I make you some or would you rather stick with your wine?'

Miranda was sure she detected a note of disapproval at her lone drinking. 'I get it,' she thought, 'I'm potentially decadent for drinking a glass of wine but the cigarettes and the occasional spliff are OK.' Jenny hesitated at the door to her room.

'Miranda, I know we said we wouldn't stay long but when you're away in Lisbon would it be, like, Ok, for me and Toby to stay on here; kind of flat-sit for you?'

Much as Miranda had hoped they would have gone by then it now seemed like a reasonable idea.

'Yeah, that should be fine. What are you planning though about where to live? You can't be comfortable in there and you will need to make preparations for the baby.'

'I reckon I'll get help from the local authority, a housing association flat or something. You know, single mother, etc.'

'That sounds fine, but what about Toby?'

'We've gone into all of that. We'd have to say I was on my own but he could still stay there. He'd need a different home address and not leave too much stuff around of course.'

She was fairly cool about the whole thing but to Miranda it seemed deeply unsatisfactory from Toby's point of view. But she knew better than to attempt anything which resembled interference.

Chapter 8

Bloomsbury

Miranda and Anni had been to an exhibition at the British Museum and afterwards wandered around the nearby streets, browsing in the occult bookshop and the store that sold Greek artefacts. They drifted over to the London Review Books for Miranda to pick up a book on the history and art of Lisbon. They were having coffee in the cafe, which was such a welcome addition to the store, when Mike called. He was in town meeting Duncan, his partner for the Patagonia trip. They were having a planning meeting for the expedition and he'd remembered she said she was going in with Anni so how about meeting for an early supper?

It sounded good and Anni, as usual, was instant agreement and seemed to have no plans for the evening. After Miranda had confirmed the arrangements with Mike, she and Anni chatted generally for a while about books. Then Anni suddenly leant over the table and switched topics.

'The other day Susannah seemed to be suggesting that I was a touch too friendly with Mike. Think she was kind of warning me off him on your behalf.'

Miranda felt an anxious stirring inside.

Anni didn't seem to require her to respond but continued, almost as if she was musing to herself.

'You know, I don't know what it is with people; they don't seem to think it's possible for a man and a woman to have a close friendship that is just that.'

Miranda nodded, unsure what to say.

And ...?

Anni picked up her coffee cup and stared into it before saying.

'Oh, she didn't push it; it was more of a heavily dropped hint and, of course, I will choose to ignore it. I need to keep friendships that are special for me.'

Anni had the habit of fiddling with her bracelets and of lazily flicking tendrils of hair behind her ear. Whereas Miranda had originally found this appealing it was now intensely irritating.

Susannah's warning to Anni showed concern for Miranda's happiness, but it was not what she wanted to hear as it was further evidence for her growing suspicion that Anni's interest in Mike was more than purely friendly. In fact, Anni had affected the dynamics of her relationship with Mike, becoming a kind of subversive presence. Did Anni really want Mike for herself? She didn't feel able to confront Anni yet she felt cowardly to let the moment pass. Was Anni expecting her to challenge her about her feelings for Mike? And what had been the point of introducing the subject? Was she saying that her feelings for Mike were simply platonic or was it a way of saying that she regarded her own emotional needs as priority and would betray Miranda if it suited her purpose. Or maybe it was an attempt to lull Miranda into a false sense of security so that she would not try to exclude her from their lives.

Suddenly she no longer wanted to be alone sitting in the cafe with Anni: she wanted to be with

Mike and to be reassured about his feelings for her so, to break up this mood, she suggested calling in at the Hawksmoor Church in High Holborn before making their way to join Mike and Duncan.

St George and the Dragon looked odd, sandwiched as it was between high buildings on a narrow rectangular piece of land. A steep flight of steps, lead up to the entrance, which resembled an Italianate palace. The pavement was not wide enough to afford a good view of the sculpted lions and unicorns crawling up the pyramid which was topped by a statue of King George 1, so it was necessary to cross the road for a better view. Once inside the church the cool, uncluttered interior and nave with clerestory windows, was a peaceful antidote both to the manic traffic outside and Miranda's own turbulent emotions. They wandered around the interior separately, Miranda taking in the details of the architecture and pausing to look at the pelican above the baptismal shell. She remembered the use of the pelican here to symbolise the communion bread and wine, as in legend the pelican was reputed to pierce its breast to feed its young with its blood.

Their walk to the gastropub took them back through the streets near the British Museum and via Russell Square Gardens to a quiet side road in the vicinity of King's Cross.

For most of the way they strolled in silence. Miranda was still uneasy about their conversation in the bookstore coffee shop and she felt wary of Anni while being grateful that it was possible to be in her company in an easy silence. For many people silence seemed to be an embarrassment or an unwelcome gap that had to be filled.

The pub was a Victorian building with vestiges of stained glass in the windows. Huge cured hams hung on hooks, chandeliers were suspended from the ceiling and a tiled mosaic was prominent on one of the white-washed walls.

The menu featured a wide range of tapas and hearty dishes cooked in earthenware bowls. It was a place where you could eat and drink comfortably without any pressure. Drinks were served in stackable duralex glasses (durex glasses as Mike and Miranda called them).

The place was busy with people struggling to get attention at the bar.

Mike and Duncan were waiting for them. They collected drinks and took them outside to enjoy the warm evening air and to give Anni the opportunity to smoke one of her tiny French cigarettes.

Twirling her glass in her usual languid manner, Anni commented, 'You know, these are classic items. This glass is called the Picardie and they're regarded as classic nostalgia; one is in a museum in Paris.'

'Don't know about French museums; they remind me of school dinners,' Duncan said.

'That's the other version – the gigoyne, which is another classic.'

'Well, quite frankly, I don't care what it's called as long as it's got some wine in it.'

After the Anglesey trip Miranda felt comfortable with Duncan immediately. She noticed again that he was a good-looking guy. He exuded energy and good health, and, although sharing Mike's philosophy of life, seemed more relaxed about it. He was excellent company and it occurred to Miranda that this could be the way out of the situation; to fix Anni up with someone. She observed Anni's reactions to Duncan and she seemed absorbed by him. She was engaging him in conversation about his climbing experiences and he appeared responsive to her attentions. What a wonderful resolution to her problem that would be. They ordered a range of tapas dishes and the signature drink of the summer months, a jug of Sangria.

Mike and Duncan were planning to attempt the North Pillar of the Fitz Roy Massif in Patagonia. It would be an autumn departure from the UK and they had allowed themselves three months to travel to Patagonia, survey the territory and choose the appropriate moment for their ascent. Mike was explaining the importance of the final preparations.

'It's not like packing for a tourist holiday. You have to consider what you have to take, what you don't need and how you're going to travel with it. There's a massive amount of tackle plus essential clothing.'

Anni was interested in their travel arrangements: she was a dedicated traveller but since the break-up of her marriage her resources had not stretched to foreign trips.

'We'll fly to Buenos Aires, then take an internal flight to a place called El Calafate where we'll have an overnight in a hotel. Next day we'll do the three-hour bus trip to El Chalten which is our base. It's a small village that just exists for tourists and climbers, and we'll bunk down in a hostel before we start the climb.'

'And when do you actually start your ascent,' Anni asked?

'It's all about weather, in Patagonia in particular,' Duncan explained. 'It can be hideously frustrating but you have to wait for the moment. Storms and ice rime are problems so you need to be open minded. The weather does become an obsession, but if it was that easy everyone would do it.'

Hearing Duncan and Mike talk with such conviction tapped into Miranda's own occasional despair at the selfish, more aggressively acquisitive aspects of Western society. Much as she had loved the nature and solitude of North Wales and recognised how much the experience had enriched her as an artist, she knew that most of her motivation and inspiration came from urban life, whether the charm of the architecture of Renaissance cities and culture, or the frantic lively buzz of contemporary London.

'If we were all content to have a little less and to take life at a slower pace, the benefits to society would be immense,' Duncan was saying. 'The real problem that we have is affluence and consumer greed. That's what being on the mountains does to you; it encourages a different approach to life.'

And then her thoughts were interrupted when a most unpleasant episode occurred. A gypsy flower seller approached their table with the inevitable red roses and began to persuade them to buy by thrusting roses at the women. After a polite refusal from all of them in turn, the woman did not move on as expected but continued to plead, becoming ever more insistent. Miranda raised her hand in a gesture of dismissal and was appalled when the woman drew even closer to her and grasped her arm. The woman's grip was firm and Miranda struggled to free herself. She detested the proximity to this woman who spoke an alien language and would not be shaken off. She was so close that she noticed the woman's long-coloured scarves and the roughened skin on her hands. As she tried again to pull away she could detect an unpleasant sickly sweet smell on the woman's skin. Finally managing to free herself, Miranda turned on the woman in rage and shouted.

'For heaven's sake go away and leave us alone. Just piss off.'

She felt instantly ashamed of her outburst and her resort to street level language but became uneasy when, instead of accepting the rejection, the woman drew even closer, her eyes narrowed and, leaning over the table she took Miranda's hand as if she was about to shake it, and began to scratch circles around her palm, all the while muttering in her own language. Releasing Miranda's hand she gave her a final venomous look and walked away.

Miranda had a panicky, fluttery feeling inside and felt slightly nauseous.

There was a brief silence, broken by Duncan's laughter.

'Well, looks like you're well and truly cursed, Miranda.'

The others laughed good-humouredly, but she felt uneasy. The woman's strange behaviour had upset her, and, apart from anything else, her palm felt hot and grubby so she excused herself to go and wash her hands and then suggested that they move inside to eat. Once in the pub interior she was able to relax and dismiss the episode as a mere irritation.

Chapter 9

Lisbon

Lisbon was unique as a Western European city: thought to be the oldest European city after Athens, and steeped in the magic of its Moorish heritage, it offered an intoxicating display of intricate architecture. It was an intriguing city of contrasts with classical grand boulevards only streets away from the non-renovated, dilapidated urban decay that characterised the precipitous cobblestoned streets and alleys that led away from the central grid system.

It might be the poorest country in Western Europe but it made up for lack of global advancement with charisma and layers of art, culture and conviviality. It was a city where people lived outside; it was energetic and vivacious but not frenetic like Paris or Rome; life seemed to be more relaxed and at a slower pace, giving time to absorb.

It was a place where Miranda could indulge her passion for architecture and acquire inspiration for her art projects. The streets were a delight with their jumble of crumbling time-eaten buildings and flashes of the ultra-modern.

The city also provided a new ingredient in the relationship of Miranda and Mike: it gave them a type of privacy. It was the first time they had been in a situation where they were alone together without the prospect of meeting friends or colleagues, the distractions of work and instant communications, and the weekly routine. Miranda relished the prospect of his undivided attention if with some concern about the intensity of being genuinely alone. She realised how little they had talked or questioned each other about what had happened before they met. They hadn't been together long enough to have any real shared history but there was between them the knowing secrecy that only lovers can share. Part of the attraction was that, as yet, there was no 'backstory'. That part had yet to be written.

Mike and Miranda found it an invigorating city. Early morning walks took them up the unrelentingly steep streets in the relative cool of the day to take in the stunning views.

It was a city of elevations; built on seven hills, the landscape soared up in steps and inclines. From the miradouros or scenic viewpoints they could look down via twisting streets into the darkened alleyways below. One of their early morning destinations was the Bairro Alto, an ambiguous neighbourhood that by day was festooned with coloured laundry drying over cobbled streets that were lined by shuttered shops and graffiti sprayed walls. But as twilight fell, a surreal change took place and it metamorphosed into an area of restaurants and bars, jazz and fado places. If they returned here at night to walk and drink they would marvel on its transformation.

Their early morning walks left them glowing and hungry as they descended to drink intense black coffee in a cafe and make plans for the day.

Miranda's romantic soul responded to the glut of baroque churches, tiled mosaics on walls, Pracas that appeared like apparitions around corners with tiny fountains and the occasional tree, and the suggestions of picturesque squalor in narrow, stepped alleyways where washing was strung on balconies and shops spilled their wares on to the pavements. The sort of squalor that was fine as long as you didn't have to live in it.

They spent the days walking, drinking in the atmosphere, finding constant things to look at. Sunshine pervaded the streets from early morning until evening. A mild breeze blew off the Tagus River and occasionally whipped up into a stronger wind. The back streets of the Baixa area provided constant fascination. Eating was fun and they enjoyed finding places to reflect their mood of the day, from minimalist restaurants with brilliant fluorescent light and waiters mesmerised by futebol on big plasma screens to dark, charismatic fado bars that seemed to have emerged from the nineteenth century.

It was a city for romantics. The all encompassing warmth meant that life spilt out on to the roads and pavements. The fact that it was built on seven hills afforded phenomenal views over the cityscape. Ancient funiculars toiled up precipitous narrow streets arriving at tree-shaded plateaus. They delved into the side streets and alleyways, occasionally startled by the vibrant graffitied walls; many of the murals were political and communicated their messages via harsh pictures and bold, challenging colours. They took pleasure in looking at the many tile mosaics and buildings painted in astonishing colours of blueberry and porcelain blue.

The old Moorish area of Alfama was Miranda's favourite haunt and one that she frequently explored alone while Mike's innate desire for heights and air took him to the highest areas of the city for the panoramic views or led him to take lengthy walks by the river.

The packed alleyways of the Alfama had a Kasbah-like layout as a reminder of its exotic past. Steep streets and stairways wound between elaborate facades which hinted at past opulence. They would meet sometimes in the Alfama when the golden afternoon light flooded the city. They found the Largo das Portas a veritable delight where they could sip drinks and look out over the Tagus River with a backdrop of historic Moorish architecture rising above.

But Miranda's favourite time of day was the early evening when the sight-seeing and occupations of the day were over. Driven inside by the intense heat and activities of the day, they often spent the last few hours of the afternoon in the hotel room. Only a short walk from the impressive Praca dos Restauradores were narrow residential streets lined by five and six storey buildings where budget hotels were jammed between local grocery stores, eclectic shops and cheap, workmanlike cafes. Tiny shops selling food, wine, flowers, caged birds and household products took over the narrow broken pavements. She had learned that these were called 'drogarias' and sold an immense number of varied products in a tiny space. Bits of masonry which had fallen from buildings frequently blocked parts of the pavements.

Here, in the Rua das Portas Santo Antao, they had found accommodation on the fifth floor of an inexpensive hotel. It was a small room with minimal furniture and a tiny balcony overlooking the street. Arriving back after a day's exploration of the town they would debate between wearily climbing up five floors or risk possible incarceration in the intimidating black wrought iron lift which was only big enough to hold two people and creaked and jolted disturbingly. In the room with the window wide open and the curtain moving softly in the breeze, they would stretch out on the bed in the languorous heat and lack of inhibition encouraged by this city which seemed to welcome and embrace them.

Their habit during this brief holiday was to leave the hotel in the evening and walk through the narrow residential streets behind the main boulevards, sometimes using the tiny elevador to reach the top of the Barrio Alto. Here they could wander past stores selling unusual artefacts and second hand books, catch glimpses of working ateliers and come across snatches of domestic life viewed through narrow doorways that opened on to courtyards. Radio noises and cooking smells drifted from open windows high above. They would end their walk in the smarter shopping area of Chiado, with its fountain and baroque church and follow the steeply twisting street down past high end stores, gift shops, small galleries, bars and cafes and a generous sized branch of FNAC.

Next to the trendy and tourist-haunted Cafe A Brasileira, a favourite with intellectuals in the nineteenth century, with its bronze statue of the poet Fernando Pessoa on the street terrace, they had discovered the Cafe Berard, an equally impressive nineteenth century bar where locals sat inside on bentwood chairs or stood at the bar to order drinks and pastries. They were amused by the elderly single women, smartly dressed with heavy make-up and abundant jewellery, who would delicately dispose of hearty pastries and cups of coffee. Young people lounged at the bar and workers would call in to purchase cakes and savouries. With so much rich sweet food, why weren't the people all fat, they mused?

Over glasses of crisp Vinho Verde and the occasional sweet pasteis de nata, they would share their separate experiences of the day and plan a leisurely evening.

Largo do Carmo

On one of her afternoons alone Miranda was sketching in the relative shade of the Largo do Carmo. Her subject was the Gothic structure of the Igreja do Carmo with the skeletal ruins of the Carmelite convent. The ruins of this fourteenth century convent stood out theatrically over the Bairro Alto district. So many of the ancient buildings in the city were ruins that remained after the terrifying earthquake of 1755 which devastated huge areas of the city. The event itself was a gothic horror and was depicted in the guide books with real terror. On a clear morning on the first of November when large numbers of the population were in churches celebrating All Saints, three massive tremors shook the city. Enormous numbers of the population were consumed by flames, crushed by masonry or swept away by tidal waves. Candles that had been lit to commemorate the Day of the Dead started fires that raged around the city for seven days. Seventeen thousand buildings collapsed. Miranda found it impossible to envisage this apocalyptic horror. It was after this that reconstruction work had begun and was yet to be completed. And yet there was so much beauty in the ruins: maybe it was this surreal quality and the haunting memories of the tragedy which gave the city its dreamlike effect, Miranda thought.

The small square of the Largo do Carmo was peaceful at this time of the afternoon and Miranda was seated by the Dolphin Fountain near a small pretty tree. She worked mainly from photographs and quick notes or memory, but sometimes took the opportunity to make a fuller sketch in her compact Paperchase pad.

The previous evening they had visited the Clube de Fado in the Alfama district. Having listened to strains of the melancholic fado music wafting down the streets of Chiado each day, they had decided to go for a live experience of the indigenous music. The Clube de Fado was a very traditional building; a sequence of spacious interconnected rooms with roughly plastered walls, and alcoves and shelves displaying traditional artefacts. Customers sat on rattan seated chairs at long shared wooden tables while the fado musicians performed in one corner of the room. It was said that fado is only successful if the listeners are moved to tears; the music, with its wistful, plaintive notes demanded attention and the receptive audience conversed and applauded in the breaks. Here they met Tom, a healthy crew-cut Australian who was on a backpacking tour of Europe but based himself in London where he stayed at the Generator Hostel in Bloomsbury, much favoured by Antipodeans. He shared Mike's interest in climbing and they quickly established a rapport, making plans to meet up when they were back in the UK. As a lone traveller Tom was accustomed to making friends rapidly and easily and entertained them with anecdotes about travel encounters. Miranda liked Tom and became aware that after some time alone with her, Mike was ready for robust male companionship.

Chiado

Returning her thoughts to the present, Miranda felt satisfied with the outlines of her sketch and was planning the materials she would use later to bring it to life as she collected her things and began her late afternoon ramble through the Trinidade and Carmo areas before going to Chiado where she had arranged to meet Mike at 6.00 pm. There was much to interest her in the shops and dwellings that she passed. She paused to study some elaborate tiles on the facade of a tall townhouse and ventured into a sculpture studio where she attempted a conversation with the owner in their shared language of French. But despite being able to read French reasonably proficiently, Miranda failed to sustain anything resembling a conversation so excused herself with smiles and a quick 'obrigada'.

Reaching the top of Chiado she calculated she had time for another visit to the Igreja dos Martires which was balanced precipitately at one side of the Largo do Carmo.

The dimness and almost total silence of the interior was a shock after the heat and noise of the streets. It was a long, narrow church with a highly vaulted interior. Banks of candles flared in front of the side altars and scents of incense wafted from the high altar. Miranda walked down the aisles, attempting to see the paintings in the side chapels but finding it difficult to discern much in the murky light. She loved the atmosphere generated by European churches and treated them like art galleries, respecting the beauty and achievement but divorced from any deep seated religious belief. It was disappointing that English churches had to be so sterile and lacking in comfort. To Miranda they almost always felt cold and lifeless, unlike their Mediterranean counterparts where there lingered a sense of past events and something which was unfathomable. She lit a candle at the altar of St Anthony, having developed a fondness for the saint after realising he was the patron saint of Portugal, although he had been colonised (stolen even) by the Italians.

An evening Mass was about to take place at the Lady altar: a few parishioners had assembled and she listened for a while to the chanting murmur of the prayers before making her way to a side exit to avoid disturbing the congregation. Pushing aside the heavy curtain she negotiated a particularly insistent and surly beggar who was firmly ensconced in the doorway, and reaching the road felt dizzy with the heat. No doubt the effect of limited food and too much time on concentrated sketching in the sun. Trying to avoid the sun she turned left and into a cool side street. It was devoid of interest so she continued on and then found herself in a long alleyway. Assuming it would lead straight back to the main street in Chiado she followed it until it wound to the right and then discovered that she was in a cul de sac with some abandoned buildings at the end. They must have originally been smart town houses and, despite their present dilapidated state, there were resonances of former elegance in the grill work on the window frames and the intricately carved motifs on the walls. Miranda recalled an exhibition she had seen in one of the small private ateliers which had featured a series of black and white photographs of similar windows in empty dwellings. 'Finestra Morta' it was called. She liked that idea; 'Dead Windows', and thought she could do something similar for one of her contemporary icons. Stepping back on to the deserted street to get a better view to hold in her mind, she noticed a movement to her left. Turning to look towards the exit from the alleyway she saw a black dog; motionless, apparently alone, and staring at her. Miranda was afraid of dogs, unless they were cosy domestic English dogs on leads and being taken for family walks in parks. But to be confronted by a lone dog in a deserted alley of a foreign city was a fearful event. It was a sleek-looking dog; certainly not a stray. It looked like a Rottweiler or some other such potentially vicious breed. It must have escaped from a nearby building, no doubt a guard dog trained to attack on sight. She was terrified and looked desperately around for any sign of human presence and possible help. Nothing. The street was silent. The buildings were either abandoned or firmly shuttered. There were no shops or cafes or half-open entrances with glimpses of courtyards. She tried to remember advice she had been given about dealing with a lone dog. A dog-owning friend of hers had said, 'if you're afraid don't make eye contact: they'll either think you want to play or that you're challenging them. Avoid looking at them and don't let them see that you're afraid.' There was no need for this dog to see that she was afraid, he must have been able to smell her fear, and he was beginning to walk slowly towards her. She had no choice but to walk past it; there was no other way out. Averting her gaze and staying close to the wall on the opposite side of the street, she started her slow walk in the direction of the creature.

Her palms were sticky and she could feel cold perspiration seeping from her armpits. She recalled an episode in an Ian McEwan novel where a woman had confronted a group of black dogs and had fought them off with a stick. But she didn't have a stick, and anyway would have been far too scared to wield it. Even in her state of terror the artist in her appreciated the heavy studded collar that the dog was wearing. No; it had crossed the street and was now walking behind her. Miranda quickened her pace; surely only a few steps to safety. Then she felt heavy paws on her shoulders and hot, sickly sweet breath on the back of her neck. Dear God, the thing was on her. She was shaking uncontrollably and felt incapable of action.

She could feel the contents of her stomach rising up and was convinced that she was going to be sick. Then there was a noise of a nearby door banging and the dog's paws slithered off her shoulders. She walked faster without looking and as she reached the end, turned to see the dog still standing there, looking bemused, if anything. Turning, she ran until she finally emerged on to the main street. Here it was all lively, animated early evening civilised activity. So much normal and secure life was going on while she was being terrorised in a darkened alley. It reminded her sickeningly of the incident in the corridor with Joel when the world seemed to be going about its business while she confronted a private terror.

Now: to find Mike at the cafe and unburden herself. She expected to see him sitting outside at a table nursing a beer and looking for her, wondering vaguely why she was late. Café A Brasileira was manic as usual with people grouped near the bronze statue of Fernando Pessoa, Lisbon's significant poet. And all the tables outside Cafe Berard were occupied. Of course, there was nowhere to sit out here so he would have gone inside to wait for her. She brushed past people blocking the entrance in her haste to find him and sought out their favourite seat. He wasn't there; and how she hated the sight of the elderly woman who was sitting at their table calmly spooning sweet custard into her mouth. She looked like a satisfied well-heeled woman finishing a day's shopping. Not someone alone in a strange city who had just been almost mauled by a vicious dog and had now lost her lover. Where the hell was he? Out on the pavement again Miranda scanned the crowds in the Rua Garrett which descended through Chiado. No sign of him there so she retreated to the fountain further up in the Praca and tried his mobile. No response; she was cut off immediately. She tried texting but with no result. Anything could have happened. He could have collapsed somewhere or been attacked and could even now be lying in a Lisbon hospital, unable to communicate. No one knew who she was and he wouldn't be carrying anything to link her to him, or of where they were staying. The routines and restrictions of everyday life in England now seemed remarkably comforting: that there were people who knew what you were doing, who expected you at certain times and places, and would wonder what had happened. But here, it was Mike and Miranda alone. A more rational side of her took over and she decided to spend some time looking around the nearby shops, pretending that there was a reasonable explanation; he was only a bit late, and soon he would appear. Although in fact he was already a good half an hour late. She'd give it another half an hour and then go to the hotel and enlist the help of Maria, the friendly middle-aged proprietor who spoke very good English. She would understand and help her.

Now that she had taken control and given herself a plan she felt better and made her way to a small, cramped store where she had seen old black and white postcards of city scenes. She would buy some of these before resuming her search. She followed the street on its winding downward curve to the bridge over the road which linked the elaborate Victorian elevador to the Carmo area where she had been earlier. But he didn't seem to be in the groups of people walking upwards. Retracing her steps she noticed a pretty carved wooden box in an upmarket gift shop and contemplated going in to ask the price, but decided that would have to wait until she was in more of a relaxed mood. Further attempts to contact him by mobile were futile and now she was once more approaching the cafe, forcing her way through people queuing at the bar and scanning the interior. He was sitting at their regular table, a beer in front of him and the custard-eating woman nowhere in sight.

'Where were you? I was so worried? Why didn't you answer my calls?'

'OK, calm down. And I would like to point out that we agreed to meet here and when I got here you weren't.'

'That's because I was out there searching for you. Obviously you weren't concerned enough to do the same for me.'

'Because there wouldn't have been any point as I didn't know where to look.'

'So you would just have sat here drinking beer instead?'

'In the fullness of time I would have moved on and begun to investigate but I think one-hour late is a bit quick to label you as a missing person. I would have assumed that you had forgotten the time and that you were happily engrossed in your churches or old bookshops.'

'In fact, I was in a deserted alley about to be attacked by a vicious dog; a Rottweiler or something.'

'Hey, that's a bit strong, surely?'

'It's true; he jumped up and put his paws around my neck.' Reliving the experience made her feel shaky.

As they stood by the cafe table Mike embraced her and she felt a warm, relaxing feeling seeping through her limbs. Then as she turned to sit down he said.

'God, you're right. I can see the marks on the back of your T-shirt. Come on, sit down and I'll get you some wine.'

Once their glasses of Vinho Verde had arrived he continued.

'And in answer to your multitude of questions I met Tom this afternoon, we took a longish walk by the Tagus and ended up in a riverside bar. Then I had to race back here to meet you and got delayed in a queue in FNAC.'

'Why, for heaven's sake, did you have to go to FNAC?'

'For this, and he handed her a small package containing a CD of fado music.'

She gulped almost half of her glass of wine, reached across the table to take Mike's hand and then told him about the pleasanter aspects of her day.

'Thanks for getting me this.'

'Actually, it's a bit of a peace offering.'

'For being late?'

'Not exactly; it's a bit more significant than that.'

And then the blow fell.

'I need to move on.'

'What do you mean?'

'I've got the chance to go with Tom to do some walking and leisure climbing in Spain: it'll be good fitness preparation and I'd like to see Spain. I can change my airline ticket and fly home from Spain.'

'But what about me?'

'You'll be fine, Miranda. It's only three days until you go home anyway and you're used to the place now. You spend most of your time with your old buildings and artwork anyway so this will give you more opportunity without me interrupting.'

'I actually like you interrupting. It's great to sit like this as the end of the day and share what we've done. Bloody Tom. Why did he have to interfere?'

'He didn't interfere, Miranda. I was up for it anyway and ready to get going. This has been good, but, you know it's cultural stuff and my mind's on the expedition and widening my experiences. I'm basically a loner and sometimes I feel as though I'm being cocooned in cotton wool.'

She knew she had to accept this, and maybe he was right. She felt confused and taken aback by his sudden announcement but it might be exciting having the opportunity to be independent and steep herself in her work in this fantastic location.

'Right, so when are you going?'

'Tomorrow, first thing, so tonight it's your choice, anywhere you want to go and anything you want to do.'

The evening

It was a strange evening; bittersweet she supposed. There was the pleasure of the moment mingling with sadness that their relationship seemed to be ending plus her anxiety about spending the rest of the time here alone. And it certainly was a strange evening. The torrid heat was unrelenting as they walked over the massive Praca dos Restauradores, one of the magnificent piazzas which had been restored by the Marquis de Pompal. The soaring obelisk in the centre was surrounded by an open square paved in black and white mosaic with a wave design which reminded Miranda of an advertisement for seasickness tablets and made her feel slightly queasy. This evening a warm wind was blowing with some force and the postcard and newspaper vendors had begun taking in their wares.

Mike's mobile had bleeped with a text message while he was showering. Who did Mike know in Lisbon? Probably Tom with arrangements for the next day but she decided to check.

A brief message, 'Good luck enjoy spain A xx' and a smiley. Anni's number. Was there anywhere this woman didn't get to? It was rare that Miranda regretted a friendship but with this one she did. Was female friendship so transient?

They walked up in the sticky warmth of the evening through the Biarro Alto until they found a quiet restaurant tucked down a side street with a terrace giving evocative views over the city. They ordered drinks and once she had the courage of the wine she broached the subject of Anni, admitting that she had accessed his text message.

'How come she knew about your plans? Have you been texting her with an on-going commentary?'

'She sent me a few texts and I just let her know how we were doing.'

'How we were doing. She's that interested in me? Come on, Mike, what is this really about? There's so obviously something going on between you. People have started to drop hints and Susannah has even warned Anni off you.'

'Well, she had no right to; the meddling cow.'

'She happens to be a good friend of mine who cares for my welfare and wants to stop me making a fool of myself, although I think I've left it too late for that.'

'You know, Miranda, this is why I climb mountains; to escape from the crass pettiness of so much of everyday life. There's nobody watching you on a mountain except the people who are there to help you and work with you. There's real companionship and a bond created by mutual dependence and the need to work together for survival. Here you can feel suffocated, and that's a bit how I feel now and so I need to take this chance to go to Spain with Tom and work off some of this energy.'

'And, to answer my question about Anni?'

She knew she was being persistent but she was so steeped in it now she might as well pursue the question.

'For God's sake, I felt sorry for her. She's clearly lonely; she asked for my advice about a few things. Think she wanted someone to talk to about her divorce, ex-husband, etc. Why would I have bothered spending time with you, coming here on holiday with you, if it was all about her? You need to relax about yourself, Miranda. You're a talented woman with great prospects in your career as an artist. You don't need me to clutter things up.'

Not the response she had expected. She felt drained of energy. The hectic day, getting lost, the episode with the dog, not finding Mike and then the news that he was leaving. What had been the point? She had been too much in the world of 'What if?' and not enough in the here and now.

But for once she was just going to let go and enjoy every minute of this last evening. Looking at him in the diminishing light she thought that he was the most sexually attractive guy she had ever been with. There always had been the uncertainty and the slight hint of danger; if only she could have held on to this for longer. They ate smoky sardines and goat's cheese soaked in honey, washed down with a robust red Portuguese wine. Mike smiled and his eyes crinkled in that lovely way as he raised a glass to her.

'We've had a good time: good luck with your work.'

Those intense blue eyes were a really unusual colour. She would never trust those sorts of eyes again.

The dessert of the day was a special one for sharing, Zabaglione, which their waiter would prepare at the table. They watched while he concocted the froth of egg whites and Madeira scooped generous portions into balloon shaped glasses. It was light as air and powerfully alcoholic.

When they stood to leave the table she realised that she was extremely drunk, in part because of the time she'd spent in the heat of the afternoon sun but mainly because of the alcohol.

She stumbled a bit as they walked down towards Baixa; the wind was increasing and as they reached the hotel there was an explosive noise of thunder and a few drops of rain.

Chapter 10

Solitude and Sao Roque

There was an insistent drumming at the window; it was dark, almost pitch-like with weak light filtering through the slatted window blinds. Where was she? Miranda struggled to let her eyes get accustomed to the gloom and began to reorient herself. It was a hotel room; they were on holiday and she was here with Mike? Where was Mike? The other side of the bed was empty and the duvet had been pulled over her. What time was it? The travelling clock by the bed read 11.00 am. But it was so dark and how had she slept so long? Memories of last night's alcohol hit her as she stumbled to the window. It was pouring; vicious, heavy unrelenting rain, pounding on the roofs and cascading down the gutters. Everything was plunged in a miasma of greyness. The street below was virtually invisible in the torrents and strong winds swept the rain over the pavements and up the walls in gusts. It was tropical in its intensity. Was anyone out there? She peered into the street and saw a lone old man struggling along with a dog in tow. The shops looked deserted and the canopies over the cafes and restaurants had been pulled back. It was so dark that she needed to switch the light on to survey the room. Mike had gone; there was no evidence of him having been in the room. Then she saw the message, scrawled on a piece of hotel paper.

'I'm on my way. Didn't want to wake you. Enjoy yourself. See you on the other side. M x.'

Cryptic but clear enough. Now she actually was on her own.

She spent the day in the room working. The rain persisted all day but when it became less torrential she was able to open the shutters and allow in what daylight there was. There was a small table in the room which she moved under the window and began to work.

Solitude was often the best catalyst for creativity and once she released her mind from immediate problems she became lost in the creative process. She had often worked through the night with an insane sort of creative energy taking hold of her. There was a feeling of being surreptitious in some way; stealing time while the world slept. She was infected by some of that energy now.

She had brought a large sketch pad which she used now to try out ideas with her photographs, postcards and small items of interest that she had acquired on her journeys round the city. Her practice in the early stages of a project was to steep herself in all the things that interested her before beginning to refine and select. This part was in fact immensely enjoyable when she sought the storytelling behind the images. Resonances of the past were important in her work and she liked to feel that past events could in some way infiltrate into the present. Her reference material was spread around her; the photographs, postcards and small items she had harvested on her walks around the city, all providing stimulation. For Miranda mimesis was important, to draw on the architecture and scenes that were around her. Her intention was to lead her viewers into her drawings, using perspective, facades, exits, entrances and labyrinthine passageways to give a feeling of enclosure which could give a sense of protection and confinement at the same time. She aimed for a dream-like quality, giving the viewer the sensation of approaching a familiar destination while being aware that the unknown lay beyond. Sometimes colour, or the lack of it, played a significant part and she realised the effectiveness of using only pencil, charcoal and graphite for some of her sketches, and deliberately making them static like stage sets. People did not appear in Miranda's work. She preferred the enticement of the haunting places with silent corridors and corners that hinted at stories. Like the scenes of Hammershoi that she felt an affinity with, there was intrigue in the possibilities suggested.

By mid-morning she had the outlines of almost half of her proposed icon pieces. She was particularly pleased with her representation of one of the grill work windows and elaborate plasterwork she had seen on a building in the Bairro Alto. She decided to convey the impression of the intricate design by using some scraps of old lace, giving the work a trompe l'oeil effect.

In the afternoon she dashed out into the street and made for a bar on the corner where she had once stopped with Mike on their way back from a day out. It mainly catered for workmen and was the kind of place where weather-beaten men of indeterminate age propped up the counter with espressos and tiny glasses of some sort of grappa. Some of those workmen were around now, as well as office workers calling in for fast food. She ordered an Americano and sipped it quickly, ready for the hit of caffeine that really good coffee supplied. The barman was pleasant if indifferent and she was aware that the other male customers regarded her with possible suspicion, perhaps wondering why she had ventured into their territory. She took her coffee to a table by the window and watched the rain. In no time this city of endless sunshine and romance had become something melancholic and potentially depressing.

Her body missed the routine of morning exercise, her head still ached and swam from the previous night's alcohol and emotion, and she had a gnawing hunger inside. She bought a cheese pastry and water to take back to the hotel and returned to the room to continue working. She worked through the night with a frenetic energy, planning, sketching, writing notes and trying out ideas. At times like this she felt the art had taken her over. She left her room only twice to seek coffee in the half-deserted bars below. On an earlier foray she had collected a very cheap screw top bottle of red wine and a packet of soft almond biscuits from a late-opening supermarket which she drank and nibbled at while she worked. By 3.00 am she was exhausted but still shaking with nervous energy. Sleep was elusive and she was tormented by weird dreams where she was walking alone through a ruined city, leaves and debris blowing around her and voices whispering but with no visible human life.

Her dreams then moved into a gentler phase where she was with people. Someone who looked like Mike was holding her firmly and stroking her neck. But as he tilted her face up to kiss her, she saw blood tricking from his neck and, over his shoulder, her eyes met those of Anni's.

It was a relief to wake up and move from the sweat-soaked sheets. And it didn't take a psychoanalyst to work out what had happened: a late night, a frantic onslaught of work, red wine and minimal food. She reviewed her work and felt that she had successfully managed to convey many of her ideas on paper. There was much here that she could work on later.

From her vantage point on the fifth floor, she could observe the street life begin to resume as the sky cleared towards the late afternoon. Spread out in front of her was a collage of ideas that formed a sort of internal dialogue. Now she needed to get out on the street; be near people even if she wasn't with them. The rain had ceased and this morning the city had resumed the calm and languor that had initially attracted her. She needed to reacquaint herself with the sun, the breeze and the streets of the city.

It was odd how her perception of the city had changed. Aspects that were appealing when she had walked the streets with Mike, had taken on a different appearance. The graffiti spattered walls that had seemed so invigorating now looked depressing and ugly, the narrow back streets with crumbling plaster and uneven pavements were just poor and squalid rather than a picturesque photo opportunity and, above all, the fado music with its previous redolence of romance was now intensely painful.

She wandered without any real sense of direction and found herself navigating the steep winding streets that led ultimately to the higher reaches of the Bairro Alto. This area was being transformed from a seedy red light district but there was still enough evidence of its unsavoury past.

Her destination became the church of Sao Roque. Sao Roque was a superb example of the baroque art that she was using for inspiration. The plain white facade of this small church belied the splendour within. The ceiling was densely painted with frescoes and opulent use of ornamentation was everywhere. The eight side chapels lining the nave were crammed with art. The gem was the chapel of St John which was reputed to be the most expensive chapel in the world. It was a fantasy of embellishment, made of alabaster, lapis lazuli and adorned in gold. Miranda fed coins into a box to illuminate the chapel and stood there transfixed by the sheer excess of precious materials. At the front of the church she read the information about Sao Roque who was reputed to be the saint who offered protection from the plague.

She imagined how it must have been to live in mediaeval times with the ever present real fear of death.

There was only the mere hint of a breeze on this humid afternoon; balcony doors and windows in the narrow streets were flung wide open and she felt the need to get out of the piazza and find somewhere cool to sit.

It was possible to walk down a series of twisting staircases, past decomposing buildings and scruffy cafes to emerge on to the ultra-modern amphitheatre which swept flamboyantly to the side of Rossio Station. Spacious open air cafes lined the top layer of the amphitheatre and opposite on the lowest level was a huge flat screen to display public events. Some of the pale-coloured lozenges which made up the surface of the pedestrian area were beginning to crack and some workmen were fixing tape over the broken edges. A film crew had set up at one end of the piazza with cameras, equipment and a van dispensing drinks and snacks.

She was hot and tired and aware of suddenly being listless. She contemplated sitting at one of the cafe tables and ordering a cold drink and looked for a vacant seat. Everyone there seemed to be in couples, either pairs of friends or lovers, and she was struck by how lonely she felt. And then she saw him; sitting on one of the steps to the side of the station with a backpack at his feet and mobile phone in hand. It was Mike! Had he changed his mind or been delayed? Whatever, she would be happy just to see him again. She made her way over to him, expecting a smile of recognition and explanations.

He must have changed his mind. He was trying to call her. He would stay and travel home with her. They would have another fabulous exciting night. And then he put the phone down and turned his head towards her. It was a complete stranger. She felt desolate and incredibly foolish as she backed away.

How crazy. All that introspective work was interfering with her conscious mind. She needed to get a grip: she couldn't afford to wander round a strange city in a semi-comatose state. And it was worrying that she was starting to feel increasingly dizzy and weak. She had to maintain control at all costs. If only she could reach a shady part where she could sit down and deal with the faintness. It was too hot and too far to walk back up to the pavement cafe so she descended tentatively towards the bottom. There was a coffee shop in the front of Rossio Station. It was a flashy branch of the Starbucks chain so would have air conditioning and soft seats. She was almost there; only a few more steps down and she would be there. But she hadn't quite reached the bottom of the amphitheatre when she felt all control slipping gently away and then a warm darkness enfolded her. The darkness had the texture of soft but cool velvet. It was the colour of the indigo chakra that she had sometimes achieved in yoga meditation. A colour that she would like to reproduce in one of the paintings. For a while she allowed herself to gratefully sink into the darkness.

And then external things began to intrude. Was she on a beach? There were noises around her like water dripping, and far away voices. Cool air was wafting over her head.

A voice was insistently saying,

'Can you hear me? Are you English?'

She could feel someone gently shaking her. Why couldn't they leave her alone? She was relaxed and peaceful. But the voice continued, sounding increasingly anxious so she knew she had to make the effort to surface. Leaning over her was a small, thick set guy with cropped hair. His accent was Irish: not the harsh tones of Gerry Adams's Belfast but the softer, melodic sixties rock group voice of Dublin.

'Yes, I'm English and I'm OK.'

'Well, you sure gave us a shock. That was some faint. Are you ill?'

It was the Irish voice again that questioned her.

'I'm sorry: I just suddenly got tired, I've been out in the heat and I don't think I've eaten much today.'

Another voice said,
'touch of the Stendhal syndrome.'

'What's that?' She heard herself saying, although it sounded familiar.

'Oh, lack of food, too much wine, heat and exotic artwork; causes delicate young English women to faint. You know, like Lucy Honeychurch in "A Room With A View".'

And then she remembered Lucy, fainting in the piazza in Florence, but surely there was blood involved there. Someone helped her sit up and gave her a glass of water. The people helping her were part of the film crew and she gathered that they were

British. There was some discussion about calling an ambulance, and one of the Portuguese workmen had come over to the scene and had offered to do that. But she was determined not to be hauled off to some alien hospital with no one she knew to assist her.

'Well, we're not letting you walk off in that condition and you said you hadn't eaten so we'll get you a drink and some food and make sure you're OK. You can't wander round existing on art and fresh air. You should have started the day with a full English.'

God, that sounded nauseating but she felt that a comforting cake would be good.

'I can take a few minutes break.'

It was the Irish voice.

'Come along, love, soon sort you out.'

A few minutes later she was sitting on one of those soft leather settees in Starbucks with a large cappuccino and muffin in front of her.

'Right, let's get the blood sugar restored and sort you out. Oh, and I'm James.'

James had a calming effect on her. He resembled the actor Ken Stott, if not so burly. His voice was melodic and reassuring and while they sat there he told her about his work. It was a British film crew and they were making a documentary about Portugal and its Renaissance since gaining EU membership. He operated a camera and worked freelance on whichever contracts came his way. He amused her with descriptions of his work, removing any illusion she may have had about it being a glamorous occupation. In fact, it was, as he put it 'damned hard work', often in uncomfortable or even life-threatening situations. One of his worst experiences had been when he was filming a celebrity chef preparing a gourmet meal in the galley of a 747 en route to New York. It was for a reality television programme; the idea being to illustrate the skill and ingenuity of the chef in coping with such difficult circumstances. But they proved even more difficult for James, having to cope with awkward camera angles in a seriously confined space, occasional turbulence and the unwelcome aromas of hot frying food.

'Give me airline plastic sandwiches any time after that.'

Miranda apologised for the drama of her fainting fit, and when James questioned her about whether she was travelling alone, merely said that she had been with a friend who had left to travel to Spain.

Then, as he was leaving to return to the crew, he casually asked if she'd be interested in joining them that evening for a 'cheap and cheerful' meal. Mobile numbers were exchanged and with directions given to her hotel, James said he would see her at 8.00 pm.

While they were talking they had discussed Portuguese culture and Miranda had said she felt ashamed about her lack of knowledge of Portuguese literature. She was aware of the prize-winning novelist Jose Saramago but knew nothing of the poetry. James told her about the poetry of Fernando Pessoa, a curious writer who adopted a multiplicity of pseudonyms to create a diversity of personae to express the world of his imagination. This attitude appealed to Miranda and she determined to find a copy of his poetry.

She had noticed a bookshop with English language translations near the Praca dos Restuaradores which was on her way back to the hotel. It was an easy task to find a slim paperback copy of Pessoa's 'Selected Poems'.

Back in her room things didn't seem quite so positive. Would he come?

To distract herself she looked over her work of the previous day again and felt reasonably satisfied that she could return home with definite ideas to present to Kate and Paul. Regular checking of her mobile showed no communication from Mike so she decided to concentrate on the evening ahead. She began reading Pessoa's poems, skimming through and reading bits that caught her eye. One short poem reflected her owns experience of the previous day and night.

'Suddenly a hand, part of some occult haunting,
Between the folds of the night and of my sleep
Shakes me, and I awake and in the deep
Neglect of night discern no face or movement
Then I wake from the dream mystery
And rejoice in the light.'

What a wonderfully evocative and sensuous use of language. There were ideas here that she would like to convey in a painting.

Looking out from her balcony window at 7.55 she could see James walking down the street towards her hotel. As they walked to their destination she found her liking for the city returning. They wandered along the Rua Augusta, a pedestrianised thoroughfare haunted by street vendors and entertainers. Coloured shawls were draped over balconies, a blind woman sat in one of the shop doorways singing fado with a triangle as accompaniment, and a slender young man was about to step on to a bed of nails.

Their destination was a bar near Praca dos Comercio, under the colonnades which encircled the enormous waterfront square. It was a lovely time of evening, with dusk beginning to fall and lights flickering on cafe tables. The stall holders in the nearby arcaded pedestrianised streets were still active, and the smell of roasting chestnuts wafted their way. The film crew were a lively, sociable group, engaging in heated discussions and drinking in the committed way that only the British among Europeans seemed able to do. Their choice of eating place later was a restaurant called Lisbon Tasca, in one of the narrow, crowded streets of the Bairro Alto.

'A tasca,' James explained, 'was a type of bar restaurant which served inexpensive local cuisine without frill or fuss.'

They ate salt cod, squid and potatoes and a hearty pork stew, which Miranda found it easier to avoid. The next day the crew were to move on to the historic town of Evora in the Alentejo region. After Miranda had talked about her job and current project, there was unanimous advice for her to visit the towns of Sintra and Evora to gain material.

'And what happens when this contract is finished?' Miranda asked James.

'I'm being very conservative at present. Got some work doing stuffy programmes for early Sunday evening TV: you know, religion and antiques. In the Autumn I'll be starting a long-term contract with a commercial television company filming a serialised drama in a hospital. I'll be located in London at UCH so maybe, Miranda, we could catch up some time.'

They left the others after the meal and strolled back to her hotel in companionable silence. At the hotel door James wished her good luck for the rest of her trip, planted a platonic kiss on her cheek and finished with a strong hug.

'Look after yourself.'

Climbing the stairs to her room she was pleasantly relaxed and tired after the walking, food and company, and found herself inadvertently thinking of how much she would enjoy recounting the details of her day to Mike. But of course the room was empty and Mike no longer there. Would he ever be? How much she missed his seductive charm, his passionate attitude to life, even his unpredictability. She felt hollow inside. His sudden departure had left a vacuum in her life.

Chapter 11

Sintra

The next day Miranda became decisive. If Mike could do it, so could she. She had no real desire to return to London after this short break in Lisbon. She still had weeks of her summer vacation left with no definite plans. She had expected to spend time with Mike; most of her friends and colleagues would be on family holidays or boozing and sunbathing with friends on beaches in Ibiza or Turkey. Anni, she knew, planned to work more hours in the Camden shop and visit her family who lived in various parts of the country, and, anyway, she didn't want to spend time with Anni. Nobody needed her and all she had to do was text Toby her intentions so that he wasn't concerned. She could work just as well here if she bought a few more materials and the weather was hot so purchasing a few T-shirts would be enough to extend her wardrobe. She would go to Sintra and Evora and see for herself the beauty that James had talked about. She left Lisbon with memories of the smell of fresh coffee, futebol and the amiable nature of the people.

Sintra, 'a place for romantics' the guide book called it. It was the place where, in mediaeval times, the occupants of Lisbon had fled to escape the plague, and then it became a different sort of refuge from the intense summer heat. The day trip was easy enough to arrange, a one-hour train journey from Rossio Station, giving her several hours to get the flavour of the place.

Sintra was a place for the senses and one that did much to satisfy Miranda's artistic sensitivities. The town looped around green, wooded ravines that were lush with mosses and ferns. Moorish influences were everywhere in the architecture of the imposing palaces and the castle. In the guide book that she read on the train Miranda learned that it was believed to have been a centre for cult worship; the hills were scattered with mysterious tombs and what appeared to be ley lines. There was also the presence of a strange white cloud that hovered over the palaces even on a clear day. She spent some time in the Castelo dos Mouros, the Moorish castle which reared above the old town: hidden inside the walls she explored the ruined chapel and made a sketch of the ancient Moorish cistern.

Back down in the town she wandered the streets, admiring the architecture and tile paintings and visiting some of the antique shops. The city was supplied with fresh water springs and she drank thirstily from one of the many fountains. By early afternoon she was hot and hungry, and sought refuge in a lively, cheerful basement cafe that seemed to be populated by locals, with a predominance of young people. Sintra had a mystical quality that contrasted with the more everyday atmosphere of Lisbon. Her visit had been enriching, but, sitting alone at the cafe table observing the friendly interaction of couples and groups of friends, she was made acutely aware of her isolation and of how much she longed to share these experiences with Mike.

On the train journey back she travelled with an American couple who chatted volubly about their travels and, when they arrived back in Lisbon, shook hands and exchanged names in the way that

Americans often did; was it just politeness, she wondered, or the expectation that you might actually meet again?

Evora

For Evora she planned a longer stay. She knew that the film crew would be staying in an international chain hotel just outside the city walls. James had explained that it was suitable budget accommodation with decent parking but lacked any ambience, so for her he recommended a small pensão located in the old part of town. It was inexpensive and would no doubt have more character.

The bus from Lisbon crossed the Tagus river via the ultra-modern suspension bridge and past the huge statue of Christo-Rei with arms outspread, the twin of the more well known one in Rio. They had entered the Alentejo with its flat countryside dominated by grain silos and cork-producing oaks. A strong stench of burning rubber flooded the bus soon after reaching the motorway. A paper manufacturing factory was located nearby so maybe that was responsible. It was a relief when it dissipated. At the same time the scenery improved, with fortified hilltop towns rearing up at intervals and curious mounds of cairns in the fields giving evidence of ancient burial sites.

The bus terminus was immediately outside the city walls and close to a huge outdoor mercato which stretched around the circumference of the walls and up into the town. Miranda followed the route uphill through the stalls selling cheeses, meats, fruit and vegetables and a massive assortment of pottery, arriving in the Praca do Giraldo, the focal point of Evora. Sticky with heat after the climb with her luggage, Miranda paused to take in a view of the Praca. It was built on a slope and reminded her of the Piazza del Campo in Siena (where the Palio horse race was run), although considerably less frenzied.

James was right about her hotel: the pensão was located a mere five minutes from the Praca do Giraldo and was a small family-run enterprise in a converted sixteenth-century building. Many of the original Arabic inspired features had been retained and her room, with white plastered walls, was simply furnished with a bed, table and chair and a small sofa. Moorish-style headboards added an attempt at a decorative touch.

Later in the day she went out to explore the town. Near the Igreja de Sao Francisco she saw the film crew. Would it be appropriate to approach them? It would be good to talk to James but she was uncertain about interrupting them. Would he even remember her? She hovered near the filming area and eventually he saw her. Recognition was immediate; he waved, pointed at his watch, and raised ten fingers to indicate ten minutes. Well, that was fine. She wandered into the church and returned to the square ten minutes later. James emerged from the crowd soon after, hugged her and said.

'I've got a few minutes; let's find a cafe.'

He was interested in what she'd been doing; seemed, in fact, genuinely interested. They talked about Evora and what she should try to see. She was disappointed that he didn't suggest meeting again, but tried to reason with herself that she had no right to have any expectations. She had said that she was going to spend some time in the Church. As they parted he gave her a quick hug and said 'Watch out for the Capella dos Ossos.'

She returned for a more detailed exploration of the Igreja de Sao Francisco, taking care to exit by the main entrance (she didn't want a repetition of the dog episode in Lisbon). James was right about the Capella dos Ossos next door to the church.

It was a lugubrious underground vault with light filtering in through only three small openings. The walls and pillars were made totally of bones and skulls held together by cement. There was no relief even from the white painted ceiling which was decorated with death motifs. It was a grisly sight and as she left the chapel she read the inscription over the door Nos ossos que acqui estamos pelos vossos esperamos. Fortunately, or not, she had the benefit of the English translation:

We bones, lying here bare, are awaiting yours.

An excellent antidote after that was to stroll through the narrow streets that branched out from the Praca do Giraldo. Leather shops selling shoes and handbags were prolific and there was a quirky little shop crammed with papier mâché goods where she bought gifts of decorated fans. Pottery shops with the now familiar Alentejo pottery in blue and ochre were everywhere; a useful purchase was an olive bowl with two divisions, one for olives and the other for the stones.

She spent most of the day walking outside to get a feel for the town; she walked in the public gardens and admired the remains of the Roman Temple of Diana which was situated next to the Pousada dos Loios. This was a converted convent now used as a luxury hotel. A glance through the main entrance gave a glimpse of polished floors, antique furniture and thick woven wall tapestries.

In the evening she found a small Italian restaurant 'Pane e Vino' where she felt comfortable eating on her own with her copy of Pessoa's poems for company. As she walked back to her hotel the sun was setting and the Praca was bathed in a reddish light. Thinking how much she would have enjoyed this scene in Mike's company, her thoughts were interrupted by her phone ringing. It was James: it sounded as if he was outside and breathless.

'Hi. Just finished for the day. We start early tomorrow but take a break around nine-ish. Do you fancy meeting for breakfast?'

She certainly did. He gave her directions to a pasteleria near the outdoor mercato and wished her good night.

The heat in Evora was intense; inland from the sea it felt dry and arid and Miranda missed the breeze from the Tagus in Lisbon and even the shade and coolness of the hills in Sintra. She took advantage of the early morning to walk before she succumbed to the heat so she was early for their meeting at the pasteleria. The mercato was as active and colourful as the day she had arrived, with the food stalls and fresh produce looking particularly tempting. She bought some tiny goats cheeses, thinking it might be a good idea to find a bakery later and buy bread for an economical lunch.

It was good to see a familiar face after spending the previous evening alone and it was so easy to talk to James. During their conversation his mobile rang.

'Sorry, 'scuse me. I'll just get this.'

With nothing else to occupy her Miranda half listened to the one-sided conversation.

'Yeah, Ok we can do that when I get home. Yes, but I can't tell you right now.'

The caller was persistent and James was obviously looking to close the conversation.

'Listen, Harry, can we do this later? I'm busy right now and anyway, it'll have to wait till I get back. Talk to you later.'

He smiled apologetically.

'My son; Harry. He's waiting for me to decorate his room when I get home and wants to talk about colour schemes and new furniture. Doesn't seem to realise the cost of phone calls to Europe. If he's got an idea he wants it sorted immediately.'

He was smiling indulgently but to her it was a blow. So, he had a son. Did that also mean a wife and, if so, why wasn't she discussing the decorations with Harry? Maybe they were divorced; that gave her some hope. She wanted to ask but it seemed inappropriate right now; she would wait for an opportunity when it might appear to be just casual interest.

They didn't have long together after Harry's call but as he was leaving he said. 'Listen, do you fancy joining me tonight to eat? There's a good chance we'll finish filming in the next few days and then we'll be moving on. Unless you've got plans for the evening?'

'No; that'll be great. Where shall we meet?'

'The Praca do Giraldo is probably best. There's a bar right in the centre near the fountain. See you there at eight.'

It had been an immensely satisfying day; she had been inspired enough to do some sketching and had collected some materials that she could use as reference for her icon series. Meeting James had made her feel less isolated and she was looking forward to the evening ahead with some real excitement. Late in the afternoon she visited the Evora Museum and was interested to see it had a good collection of Flemish paintings, and she had listened to some Fado music, reminding her of her final days in Lisbon with Mike. Almost on cue, her mobile beeped with a text from Mike. His usual cryptic style:

'Spain gr8 getting fit hope you had gd trip home m x.'

Well, she wasn't at home but was successfully enjoying herself without him. She did wonder whether he was only 'getting fit' or was also socialising, perhaps with other women. She was about to text back, telling him of her decision to stay but decided to leave it until later, maybe after her evening with

James. She could have had no idea that she would never get round to doing it.

The Pousada

It was easy to locate the bar that James had suggested as it occupied a large area outdoors on the Praca. He was already there when she arrived but he wasn't alone; there was a woman with him; they had glasses of wine in front of them and they were leaning over the table talking in an intimate way. As she got nearer she recognised her as Sherry, a member of the film crew she had been introduced to as a make-up artist. Sherry was tall and slim with short, smooth ash-blonde hair, very simply but effectively dressed in narrow black jeans and black T-shirt; interestingly, she didn't seem to be wearing any make-up. Her hands were unnaturally large; not long and narrow, but broad and chunky in a masculine way. They looked more suited to a type of large robust peasant woman who worked outdoors. She wore an enormous oval silver ring on one index finger. James greeted Miranda in the customary European fashion of a hug and kisses on both cheeks and Sherry raised a hand in vague acknowledgement. For a while they continued with their conversation, which seemed to be work related, making elliptical references to people and places that Miranda didn't know. This gave her time to look around the square and admire the imposing architecture of the public buildings and the decorative (if rather decayed) townhouses. It was still intensely hot and she noticed a large Portuguese woman fanning herself with a menu. That reminded Miranda that she had one of the papier mâché fans in her bag which she produced, and propping one elbow on the table, began to cool herself with it.

'That looks very fin de siècle,' James commented.

As if she had just noticed that Miranda was there, Sherry asked her about her impressions of Evora.

Miranda commented on the scooped-out bowl shape of the Praca and how it reminded her of the Piazza del Campo in Siena. The conversation veered from the horse race of the Palio to the question of cruelty to animals and then, somewhat inevitably, to bullfighting. Sherry began describing a Portuguese bullfight that some of the film crew had been to on a previous occasion.

'Do you remember, James? We'd been sitting around one afternoon drinking a few beers and Mick (one of the crew) said "How about it? Let's see if we can get tickets". And he did.'

'What was it like?' Miranda asked.

'Quite a ritual, actually. I mean for the spectators as much as the performers. They were all very dressed up, in a sort of Sunday best; we felt really scruffy. The actual fight was mesmerising; it was such an astonishing feat of horsemanship. In fact, it was like a ballet that had been skilfully choreographed. And the matadors were incredibly brave.'

'Remember they came on later,' James reminded her. 'That's in Spain. The Portuguese heroes are the cavaleiros and they taunt the bull with barbed sticks. Then the matadors come on.'

'Yes, that's right,' Sherry said. 'If the bulls are reluctant they charge with the horse and it's extraordinary, but for a moment or two the bull and horse seem to merge and become one.'

'The horses are specially bred for this activity and they perform some elegant dressage type movements. And in the one that we went to the whole thing was done in such an enclosed space.'

'It was great from a spectating point of view,' James pointed out, 'but must have increased the risk to the people involved.'

Miranda wanted to know how they felt about the moral aspect of it.

'Isn't it going to be banned in Spain?'

'Strangely, when you're there, you don't actually think about that, or I didn't.' James said. 'It was a bit like joining a club you'd always disapproved of, only to find that you got swept up in the atmosphere. The bulls don't get killed in a Portuguese bull fight; in fact, a policeman sits next to the president of the fight to make sure that doesn't happen.'

'But ...?' (Miranda's only knowledge of bull fighting came from reading Hemingway and studying drawings by Picasso.) 'Wouldn't the bull be maddened after all that taunting and wounding?'

'Yeah, it was interesting what happened,' Sherry said. 'When they'd kind of finished with that bull they introduced some white bulls (females we were told) that gathered around it and sort of escorted it out from the ring. At least I think that's what happened but my memory's got a bit cloudy at that point. Do you remember, James?'

'Not sure, we'd had more than a few beers earlier and it was very sultry so I'm hazy about the specifics.'

'Anyway,' Sherry said to Miranda. 'You ought to go; there's a ring quite near Evora at Regengos. I'll take you some time.'

That seemed highly unlikely, but Miranda agreed anyway.

Sherry checked her watch and signalled her intention to go. Much as she'd begun to be absorbed in the vividness of Sherry's anecdote, it was a relief to Miranda that they were apparently going to be left alone.

'Now then, Miranda,' James said, smiling as though he was about to share a secret. 'Are you ready for an interesting experience?'

'Sure, that sounds intriguing.'

'You mentioned when we met for coffee this morning that you'd like to see around the Pousada, so, I've booked us a table there for dinner tonight. I've been before and it's quite an experience. Oh, and as I didn't ask you about this and I don't know your budget, it's on me.'

That sounded splendid. And Miranda was thankful that she'd chosen to wear her only decent holiday garment, a knee-length black linen shift dress and the scarab choker that Mike had given her.

The Pousada dining room was in the convent cloisters, kept in their original state except for the addition of a glass dome over the garden area, no doubt to prevent birds from flying randomly on to the guests eating below. Tables were arranged separately down each side of the cloister with discreet gaps in between. It was, of course, cool in here after the intense heat outside. It was also rather like eating in a church as there was a hushed atmosphere, broken only by conversation too quiet to eavesdrop and the noise of heavy cutlery engaging with china. Food was brought to the table on huge metal platters and served with reverence from a side table. The result of all the formality was that the food was inevitably cold but the sense of occasion certainly suited the surroundings. James suggested that they try some of the local specialities. Acorda was a soup originating from a peasant recipe. Based on stale bread it resembled a type of porridge flavoured with garlic, salt and fresh coriander. To elevate the status of the dish for an up-market restaurant it was served with a poached egg floating on top and tiny dishes of cheese and olives. It had an intensely strong flavour and as an antidote they had ordered fresh asparagus with mayonnaise. The wine was local Borba wine; red and full bodied and very alcoholic.

While they were eating, with the wine giving her courage, Miranda introduced the topic of James's family.

'Do you have any other children?'

'No, just Harry.'

'How old is he?'

'He's fourteen; a pretty bright kid, good at music and maths and history. He enjoys academic study but he's a bit naive socially. I'd say he's not exactly street wise. He thinks he's taking care of the house while I'm away but he's too young to leave alone so my mother is staying with me.'

Mother, Miranda considered. So where was his wife? Divorced, perhaps. She asked tentatively.

'So, what about your wife or partner? Does she work away as well?'

For the first time since she'd met him, James seemed to withdraw into himself and his answer was strange.

'Harry's mother died when Harry was five.'

Harry's mother. Not my wife or my partner, and no name. How odd to identify your wife or girlfriend only as the mother of your son.

The expression on his face made it impossible to continue this line but a safe topic might be Harry himself.

'It must be difficult to make arrangements for Harry when you travel so much.'

'Oh, he's at boarding school in term time. Loves it, as it happens.'

And then, with that smile of his, as though he understood the motive behind her questions.

'What about you? Family? Partner? I notice you're not wearing a wedding ring.'

How observant. She didn't think most men would notice.

'No, not married and no children.'

'And no current partner?' He raised his eyebrows in surprise.

'No, at least, there was, until recently, but that seems to be over. It's a bit complicated.'

The conversation moved on swiftly and they decided to sample the local dessert of Elvas plums. These were huge bottled green plums served marinated in some fiery alcoholic liqueur.

'These are something else,' Miranda said.

'Yeah,' James agreed. 'I'm not a dessert person but wanted you to try this.'

Mike had become her standard for what a man should be like. She had assumed it would be hard for anyone else to match it but being with James was a totally different experience. Mike was not a person you could possibly ignore: he was all physical and mental energy; he talked quickly and confidently and even when sitting in a casually relaxed manner he looked alert and active. Mike talked a lot; about climbing, his fellow climbers, his thoughts and opinions about contemporary society, and his preoccupations in general. And then he would pause, look carefully at Miranda and ask her in a quieter, more thoughtful tone about how she was feeling, what she thought of something, or what she would like to do.

James was more contemplative. Like Mike, he had an energetic and enquiring mind but he was less opinionated and more willing to listen to the views of others. He asked more questions and seemed genuinely interested in Miranda's life and her work. They found many subjects to talk about; the films James had been involved with, the people he'd met, Miranda's art, and their shared love of Lisbon.

'Now, what about a strong black coffee?' James suggested.

'Good idea; I need to at least attempt to sober up before the walk back.'

Then her phone rang. The noise reverberated with an embarrassing volume around the cloister. By the time Miranda had retrieved it from her bag it had gone to answerphone.

Maybe it was Mike? If it had been she wished she'd got to it on time. It would boost her confidence to talk to him while she was enjoying a boozy night out with a really pleasant man.

But it was Toby's name displayed.

'Where are you? Mum's in hospital. She collapsed. Don't know what. Might have been heart attack.'

Oh no, not her mother. And her immediate reaction of panic was overtaken by a horribly selfish thought. Why did it have to be now? If only she'd left her phone in the hotel she wouldn't have found out until she got back and could at least have finished off this evening with James.

She couldn't get a response to her calls to either Toby or her father. There was nothing for it anyway except to return home.

James went back with her to her hotel and stayed while she used their internet to rebook her flight. The first available one was mid-morning which, theoretically should have given her enough time to catch the bus back to Lisbon but Miranda had an innate suspicion about the reliability of public transport so she arranged for a taxi; no doubt at great expense but she would deal with that problem later.

She so wanted to spend more time with James but common sense told her she had to pack.

'Thanks for a lovely evening. I've really enjoyed it.'

James was considerate. 'Try to get some sleep. Have a safe journey and my best wishes. Hope your mum has improved by the time you get home.'

Another warm hug and then he was gone.

The Airport

By the next morning it had still been impossible to reach either Toby or her father so Miranda had to board before knowing what had happened with her mother. It was an incredibly difficult two hours and she was impatient for the plane to land. Once at Heathrow she called her father and at last got through.

'Miranda. We've been trying to reach you.'

'Yes, I know. Didn't you get my messages?'

'Don't know. Haven't checked my phone. Too worried about your mum. Toby didn't seem to know where you were. Said you were off on holiday but thought you should have been home by now. He said he'd even tried some friends of yours but they couldn't help either. You might at least stay in touch, Miranda.'

'OK, Dad, but what about Mum?' With her patience rapidly running out. 'How is she? Was it a heart attack?'

'No, it seems not. It was some sort of heart fibrillation; missed beats. Could have been caused by stress but she's been told to watch her weight.'

'Is she still in hospital?'

'She's coming home today; they kept her in to do some checks. Anyway, I'm going there now to collect her. But we would both appreciate it if you'd come up to see us.'

'Right, I'll do that now. Be with you later on this afternoon.'

It wasn't worth going back to her flat so she took the train directly into central London and bought a ticket for her journey home to Sheffield.

Sheffield

Her mother was sitting up in bed and looking cheerful. There were the usual complaints about Miranda's lack of communication and the fact that she was always too busy with her own life to visit them. She did feel guilty, briefly, but the guilt was quickly replaced by irritation at the thought that it hadn't actually been necessary for her to come home.

She always felt oppressed in the family home; a sort of desperation seized her and she wanted to leave and go straight back to London. But her father wanted attention and asked if she would do various chores for him and cook for them that evening. Once she got started she actually began to enjoy the activity but as she was clearing up in the kitchen she thought with regret of how she could still have been in Evora with James. If she had made phone contact with her father maybe she would have stayed and delayed this visit home.

There was mince and potatoes in the kitchen so she prepared a shepherd's pie. She knew better than to make the sort of dish that she would have served to friends. When she had done this in the past her father commented darkly that he was 'not keen on this modern stuff'. She couldn't, however, resist adding some grated cheese to flavour what she regarded as nursery food. The problem was that to unwind she could really do with a glass of wine and her parents were virtually teetotal, except for the inevitable sweet sherry to serve guests at Christmas.

An excuse was needed. She invented an errand at the local 7-Eleven store and while she was there picked up a half bottle of red wine. She took her mother some food in bed and then ate in the kitchen with her father. He accepted a half glass of wine and she relaxed and chatted a bit about some of the interesting things she had seen in Portugal. He didn't seem too disturbed when she mentioned needing to return to London the next day but just said.

'Thank you for coming. Try to make it a longer visit next time.'

Chapter 12

Camden Town

Miranda always felt there was something slightly unreal about returning to home base after a time away and accepting that routine life had been going on despite her absence. She ran into Julian when she got back to the flat with some complaints (or observations, she wasn't sure which) about Toby and Jenny's domestic routine while she had been away. So, they were still there. Little attempt, if any, had been made to prepare for her return. Toby had taken over the living room with books, papers and CDs spread randomly around, and the kitchen bore witness to unwashed dishes and things out of place. Toby was there but not Jenny as she was spending some time with her mother to escape from the confines of the flat and to be 'pampered' as her mother put it. It was obvious from Toby's face that he was finding it a struggle and Miranda had been aware before she left for Lisbon that there were strains in the relationship: raised voices, slammed doors, and she was convinced that she had once noticed what looked like bruises around Jenny's face and neck. She did love her brother but frequently wanted to scream at him. Too much time together in a claustrophobic environment and there was inevitable conflict.

Toby had developed an attitude like many young men where he adopted an authoritative tone with women and seemed utterly confident in his own beliefs and opinions. There were some advantages to this as he was willing to organise and make decisions but on the negative side he was all too ready to engage in fierce arguments if his values and ideas were challenged. For Toby, there was only black and white; no compromising, negotiating or shades of grey. He stalled her impending complaint by an apology for the untidiness and a persuasive sounding guarantee that he was about to clean it up.

'Any mail for me?' Miranda asked.

'Yeah, on your table, and Mike stopped by while you away; said he was home earlier than expected and he'd sublet his room so could he crash for a couple of days. Didn't think you'd mind.'

She didn't mind. In fact she felt a thrill of excitement by the fact that he'd been there while she was away.

'No, of course that's OK. Where did he sleep?'

'In your room.' Toby looked puzzled.

'Did he leave anything for me?'

'Not sure: I don't go into your room.'

Her room, unlike the rest of the flat, was mercifully tidy. Her eyes fell on the life drawing of Mike which she had hung on the wall at one side of the bed. She missed him in a way that made her ache. She thought back to the intensity of the time she had spent with him as she unpacked and then saw the message and tiny package on her dressing table.

Picked this up on an antique stall in Spain. Thought you'd like it.

It was a tiny miniature featuring an elegant woman, probably an eighteenth-century Spanish aristocrat. It was ceramic, surrounded by delicate gold filigree. He was still thinking about her then.

With renewed hope she showered and changed and was aware of Toby shouting something about food. Clearing towels from the shower room she picked up a couple of coloured bangles that were lying on the floor. Must be Jenny's. They looked familiar. And then she remembered where she had seen them; she was almost certain they belonged to Anni. What did that mean? That Anni had been here with Mike, or simply that she had dropped them on one of the many occasions when she had been in the flat. She could, of course, ask Toby, but did she want the answer?

Toby was in good brother mode and made an effort by buying a takeaway and suggesting they eat together. They made conversation about Miranda's trip (taking care not to mention Mike's disappearance) and Toby was animated about his job and thought it might become more permanent. He had printed off a couple of reviews he had written and Miranda had to admit that they were good: she didn't know or understand the music he wrote about it but the prose was fluid and lively. She tentatively raised the topic of Jenny and he admitted that things were not good between them; too many arguments and no real agreement about anything. Jenny, he felt, was too passive and self-absorbed. The problem was, he claimed, her overbearing and dominating mother. But he was so excited about the prospect of the baby and very much wanted to take on the responsibility.

'But, hey, the good news for you is that one of the guys I'm working with has offered me a room in his house so I'll be moving out soon and you can have some peace.'

'And Jenny?' Miranda ventured to ask.

'It's up to her. If she wants to stay with her mother until the baby comes that's fine and by then I hope we can afford a flat.'

Privately Miranda felt that staying with her mother was probably Jenny's best option. A room in a shared house with music-orientated guys didn't sound exactly marvellous for a new baby, but Toby had always adopted an impractically positive approach to life, with the expectation that once he had an idea or a plan it should work, simply because he wanted it to. And, despite the numerous setbacks he had already encountered, he maintained this dream-like attitude.

Later that evening Miranda began sorting out the artwork she had completed in Lisbon. Arranging it on her work table she noticed her Taschen diary. How strange? Surely it wasn't possible that it had been there all the time; she would have found it.

'Toby, I've found my diary. You know; the one I lost that I was going on about for so long. Do you know how it got here?'

She didn't really expect a positive response but Toby knew the answer and it was one that gave her much cause for concern.

'Oh, yeah, forgot about that. One of your students brought it round. Said he had found it in his own stuff after the end of term. Must say, he was a real pain in the butt. Said he wanted to give it to you and when I said you weren't here he kind of hung around for a bit, looking at things.'

'Did he say who he was?'

'No, but I recognised him: it was the weird guy who was hanging around here a while ago asking if you lived here.'

Oh, God, not Joel. To think that he had read her diary, gone through it and found out details of her life. No wonder he knew where she was all the time. And, if he had read it and noticed her holiday dates he must have known that she was away from home when he returned it. What did he want?

She leafed through the diary to remind herself of the contents and felt a mixture of rage and embarrassment when she saw what he could have read. Not content with attempting to attack her, he had tried to get into her private thoughts. She couldn't bear to look at the diary and threw it in the bin.

There were various emails and answerphone messages including an urgent sounding email from Anni.

'Hi Miranda, got some news for you. Ring me when you get back and we'll meet A xx.'

Did she want to meet or even talk to Anni? Well, she couldn't avoid her for long, but Miranda felt that tonight she would simply stay in the flat, reflect on her travels and the work she had completed.

She was still sorting out her work and planning revisions of her drawings when Toby returned from his evening bar job which he had kept going at the weekends. For once he actually looked at her work and seemed interested, or maybe just wanted someone to talk to.

It felt odd to be back on familiar territory yet without the regular routine. Essential tasks took over at first; clearing up the flat, taking her work round to the gallery to show Kate and Paul, and then, when she could delay no longer, she called Anni. She was relieved when she got the answerphone and could simply leave a message and delay talking to her. Kate and Paul had loved her ideas and were prepared to devote one wall of the gallery for displaying her icons, plus some text with biographical information and a contribution from Miranda herself in the form of a brief artist's statement. She was delighted with their response to her work but underlying everything was a queer empty feeling and a sense of loss.

She worked at her table by the window in the late afternoon, listening to a CD of Elvis Costello, a sure sign of nostalgia, and she was moved as always by his rendering of 'My Aim is True'.

But again she felt the need to be among people. Once out among the buzz of late Saturday afternoon she was able to walk, look around and notice things of interest. After drifting around the streets of Camden Town, window shopping and generally observing people, she passed their wine bar 'Le Cigale' and, on impulse, decided to call in and order a glass of wine. One of the usual friendly bartenders was there. He greeted her and asked if she was alone or waiting for friends. It felt strangely embarrassing to admit that she was alone, and equally odd to be sitting at a corner table with a large glass of wine and no companion: something she often did in town or on holiday abroad but not here. But it was pleasant to sit peacefully, looking out of the window watching people outside and making plans for the return to college and resuming her own studies. Her eyes were drawn to a young couple sitting nearby. From snatches of conversation she gathered they were French, so maybe tourists or students. They were both slim with long dark hair, wearing jeans and T-shirts of no particular colour and both sporting large crucifixes on chains. Religious, Miranda wondered, or merely a fashion accessory? Despite their nondescript and rather subfusc appearances, they managed to look stylish in the way that only the French could; the English always seemed to fail spectacularly on the fashion front. Miranda sometimes mused about people who drew her attention and invented possible scenarios for them. They were holding hands and drinking lattes and talking quietly and comfortably.

She wondered how long they had been together, or even if they had just met (the similar dress style and crucifixes suggested a longer acquaintance). She asked herself questions about them. What will they plan to do later? Where will they go when they leave the cafe? Are they staying in a cheap hotel or sharing with other young people? They seemed innocently happy in their youthful love.

And she, of course, was now alone without knowing whether her relationship with Mike was definitely over. But she tried to convince herself that being alone was not a reason for misery so when she left the wine bar she called at the nearest mini supermarket to buy biscuits, cheese and red wine for the evening ahead. The staples that she liked to have by her when she settled to a long session of work.

Part of her routine was to do some preliminary activities before starting work so checking emails was a good enough occupation. It was then that she was alerted to a link to Duncan's blog.

Duncan's blog

1st post

Hi friends and climbing aficionados out there. Follow us on our blog while we prepare for our ascent of the North Pillar of the Fitzroy Massif. There are three of us on this climb: me (Duncan Crawford), Mike Matthews and Tom Kennedy. All experienced in different ways and we have completed a number of ascents but this is a first for all of us and is a real challenge. It's mixed climbing: Tom hasn't yet done much ropeless but we hope to be good tutors. We've arrived in the village of El Chalten where we've got beds in a hostel.

2nd post

Began the ascent today but only made it as far as base camp - too much ice rime and it's now got incredibly misty. Consoled ourselves before we came back down with cheese and chocolate. Will make another attempt tomorrow. There's a climbing school here and we're networking and making (we hope) useful contacts.

3rd post

Not possible today either - second attempt had to be aborted; more ice rime which can make for scary climbing. At least we are comfortable in the village and meeting interesting people here but really keen to get going. People ask me why I climb and all you can say is that it is addictive and obsessive. When bad things happen and you go through moments of heart-slamming terror you say you'll never do it again, but even as you're saying it, you know that you will be back. The aching beauty of the snow is a compulsion and the total deadness around you becomes seductive, but you're always alert for the breaking of the silence by the dreaded crack of the avalanche.

4th post

A bit about El Chalten for those of you who are interested. It's a place that only exists for tourists and climbers and it's relatively cut off from civilisation. From the village you get fantastic views of Cerro Fitzroy. The village is fairly basic with one ATM machine and limited cell phone reception but as you can see we've got up to speed internet connection in our hostel. There are climbers here of all nationalities to talk to here. The locals are friendly, including the dogs that seem to roam everywhere. We're eating beef, drinking red wine and trying to pick up some Spanish.

5th post

We've now spent four days in the village wandering around, getting to know the local culture and having a few beers with members of the climbing school at night. That's OK but we are becoming stir crazy and there's only so many consoling trips you can make to the chocolateria.

6th post

It's decision time. We need to go for it or wait it out until next season. Keep checking weather reports for possible storms and what other people are thinking about the weather and doing while they are waiting.

7th post

Looks like we're on our way. Some possibility of a snowstorm but it's all clear at present so tomorrow looks like being our last chance to make an ascent. Wish us luck.

There were no more posts after that so maybe they had been successful and begun the climb.

Duncan had posted a few pictures of them and of the village they were staying in. Miranda found it painful to look at Mike's smiling face and to see how enthusiastic he looked. She recalled times when he had shared his enthusiasm with her, and although he had hurt her, she had to admit to herself that she longed to be with him again.

Scrolling down the rest of the emails and deleting spam her finger hovered over a possible junk message with no subject, but then she began to read it. It began like a piece of reportage.

'Two paintings by Munch were stolen from the Munch Museum in Oslo. They were 'The Scream' and 'Madonna'. Why those two paintings? One of them dealing with mental torment and the other the painter's fascination with the erotic power of women.

And then it got personal. What do you think, Miranda? Do you agree that his female poses eroticise women?

Another Munch fan.

She read it several times trying to make sense of it. There was an anonymous hotmail address: it was not junk but was definitely meant for her. What's more, some of the expressions were familiar. Yes, she now recalled an episode in class when she first introduced Munch's paintings and she had referred to the Madonna/Whore syndrome in many depictions of females. She had, in fact, used the word 'eroticise' and one of the students had asked her what it meant. She had become accustomed to the lack of sophistication in the vocabulary of many students but instead of despairing of it as many tutors did, she saw it as an opportunity to enrich their language, and on their part they enjoyed finding new words and incorporating them into essays.

This, however, was not intended for fun and felt sleazily suggestive.

She deleted the email and cleared the whole deleted section as if cleansing herself.

Occasionally there had been cases of cyber bullying with her college students and now she understood how demeaning and frightening this could be.

She believed in making herself available to her students and had given them her email address so that they could send work or contact her with questions if they were having concerns.

Horribly, she suspected that Joel had written this, and it made her feel as queasy as she had when she realised he had read her diary.

Anni and Pete

Anni had been animated on the phone.

'I've met someone, Miranda. I joined an internet dating agency and had a couple of wasted meetings but then I met Pete and it just felt right, straight off.'

'That's great. Tell me about him.'

'He's a bit older than me; mid-forties. He used to be a rock musician and still plays guitar a bit but now he's got a photographic business with a small studio; portrait photographs, weddings, that sort of thing. Anyway, he's asked me to join him in the business and work with him advising and doing some meeting and greeting. So, I can leave college, which will be a relief because I was getting anxious about the reduction in hours they keep threatening and I can pack in the job at the gift shop as well. Now I'll have a secure source of income. Oh, and he's got a small house so I can move in with him and give up my place. I want you to meet him.'

The fact that this had all happened so suddenly came as a shock to Miranda. If Mike had still been around it would definitely have meant a feeling of relief but now she couldn't decide how she wanted to react.

They were already in the wine bar when Miranda got there, sitting near the back and deep in conversation with drinks untouched on the table between them.

Pete was charming; medium height and slightly built with hair curling over his collar and beginning to turn grey in an attractive way. He was very courteous, getting up to shake hands when Miranda came in and insisting on buying the second round of drinks when she automatically offered to get them. Anni seemed different; her languid attitude always made her seem relaxed although she rarely was, but now she appeared to be content. She sat quietly and listened attentively to Pete's conversation, occasionally adding an observation but otherwise looking serene.

So this was what she had wanted all the time, Miranda thought. A man to take care of her. It had all happened amazingly quickly but they did seem so comfortable with each other. She actually found herself feeling envious of them.

The important thing from her point of view was that Anni was now occupied and no longer interested in insinuating herself into Miranda's life, if that was what she had been doing.

She would probably never know about Anni's earlier intentions regarding Mike, and did it matter?

Mike had not even been mentioned and Anni was not especially curious about what Miranda had been doing. Then Miranda remembered the bracelets and thought she might as well return them.

'Oh, I found these in my flat. I think they're yours.'

'Yeah, they are are. Wondered where they'd got to.'

'They were on the floor of the bathroom and I'm sure they weren't there before I went on holiday.'

'I probably dropped them when I called round when you were away.'

So, she had been there. Why? But Anni clarified.

When I was clearing out my stuff at college I found a few life drawings of Toby that the students had done and thought he might like to have them.

'That was sweet of you.' And then, tentatively.

'Did you see Mike? He stayed for a bit when I was away because he's given up his room.'

'No, didn't know about that. I only saw him when he came round to my place one evening.'

Miranda let this sink in. He had taken the time to go to Anni's one evening when he returned from Spain. Anni had said it as if it was the most normal thing, so how could she ask what he wanted.

'Oh, how was he?'

'Didn't have time to talk really because Pete was there and we were going out, but it was sweet of him to give me that present.'

'Present?'

'Yeah , he said it was from Lisbon so I assumed you'd chosen it with him. Hang on, here it is.'

And she fished around in her bag and produced a soft leather purse with a drawstring top. 'It's lovely material.'

Miranda had to agree that it was and considered what his motives could have been. She recollected their conversation in Lisbon when he had assured her that he simply felt sorry for Anni and wanted to help her. Did feeling sorry for someone mean that you spent time choosing a present when you were on holiday with your girlfriend and then visiting that person unannounced to deliver the present. What had he hoped for? If his intentions were to pursue Anni then he must have been surprised to discover the existence of Pete.

Even if she was destined not to re-establish her relationship with Mike, it was unsettling to have found this out and she would have preferred not to have known.

And then the things started to arrive: cheap, tacky items; the sort of objects that could be picked up at market stalls or funfairs. They came by post in anonymous brown envelopes with her name and address printed clearly in black felt tip pen. There was a black skull on a chain, a luminous plastic key ring and, worst of all, a hideous cardboard mask; a dark face with empty eye sockets. The postmarks were blurred and there was no indication of the origin of these objects. They arrived on alternate days over the course of a week. The first one Miranda ignored, even though she felt uncomfortable about receiving this unsolicited object which was far too nasty to be a gift and could not be a promotional offer as the envelope did not contain a compliments slip. But when the second and third items arrived she had to admit that she was scared.

It was no doubt just an unpleasant prank but this invasion of her privacy made her realise how vulnerable she had become. If Mike had been here he would have dismissed it as a stupid childish joke and they would have got on with their busy lives. But now she was not so occupied and she had time to dwell. Even Toby would have helped to defuse her anxiety. His chaotic presence in her flat had irritated her but now she would have welcomed his company. If she had still been close friends with Anni she would have told her about this, Anni would have come round to the flat where they would have got tipsy and laughed about it.

It occurred to Miranda that she had never before been on her own for any length of time, and now she felt incomplete without Mike or someone to take his place.

Chapter 13

The College

It was the start of the new term. Miranda's rhythms of life were in correspondence with the academic year when she felt a sense of rebirth and new energy. This was the time of year when she made plans and what, for her, were the equivalent of New Year's resolutions. She took the tube the first day back and after crossing the Euston Road looked back at the facade of St Pancras, the nineteenth-century Gothic fantasy dreamt up by Gilbert Scott which was now housing a prestigious hotel and luxury apartments. It seemed incongruous in that setting with its ornate windows, turrets and soaring clock tower. The most startling feature being the colour of the terracotta bricks and the elaborate carved stone dragons and angels. She had seen a total transformation of this area since she had begun living in London. She remembered the original squalor and griminess of King's Cross and the areas inhabited by glue sniffers, drug addicts and prostitutes. Some of the griminess remained in side streets off the main thoroughfares where sordid looking hostels and grubby hotels still existed, but they were being overtaken by coffee shop chains and smart buildings, like the Gagosian art gallery.

The station itself was now a light, clean, airy space with its underground mall of high street chains, cafes and food stores, while the external canal-side areas now featured restaurants and student activities at York Place.

Walking to college she mulled over her plans to set up a website to advertise her artwork. Meeting the new students was exciting and also important and this was an opportunity to find out about them and to establish herself in the dual role of tutor and friendly mentor. Some of her enthusiasm was diminished however by the start of term faculty meeting with Angela and Malcolm at the end of the day. They announced, with ill concealed relish, that funding had been cut, some reorganisation was necessary and compromises and sacrifices would need to be made.

The sanitised language did nothing to disguise the fact that in simple terms, hours or even jobs would be cut. Voluntary redundancy would be offered to any suitable candidates. Private appointments were made with those tutors who would be directly affected. Miranda was disconcerted when she was asked to stay for a 'brief' interview after the meeting. Malcolm and Angela got straight to the point. Student numbers for the foundation course had fallen this year and it was felt (they didn't say by whom) that Miranda's element of the course was in some ways an extravagance and could be incorporated into other areas. So, initially, her hours would need to be reduced while the course was being phased out. She knew instinctively that their professional jealousy had resurfaced and that this was an ideal opportunity to gain vengeance. There had been an acrimonious confrontation before the end of term when they had challenged her over the amount of freedom she was giving her students over decisions about their work. They were not, of course, able to criticise the results, which were generally very good. She defended the quality of the work and explained the reasons for her approach but they insisted that she spent too much time nurturing the interests of individual students. They acknowledged that this was time consuming and that it had been Miranda's choice to do this, but was, they said, unfair if students in some areas were given more attention than others. A corporate system had to be followed and, as they pointed out, not all the faculty tutors had the leisure for this type of approach. It was the word 'leisure' that infuriated her. She was generous with her time and regarded that as part of her commitment but she resented the implication that she had nothing else to do with her life. Rage was building up inside her but it was an inarticulate rage that she knew would be self-defeating if she let it erupt. She was furious at the paradoxical nature of their argument but knew the pointlessness of confronting them and taking them on. They had the control and were determined to use any means to lever her out.

Then a feeling of numbness swept over her and she realised that this would be her prompt to find a way out. She had no idea how complicated it was all to become.

Miranda had gone through a total range of moods after the confrontation with Malcolm and Angela. As a reaction she worked late at college in a sort of frenzy, sorting out files, completing all the start of term paperwork, planning sessions with her students. She was energised by fury; she knew she was good at her job and they were trying to suppress her, so by working like this she could at least satisfy her own standards. By Friday at the end of the first week, everyone was at a low point and Sue suggested an after work drink. They congregated in one of the Irish pubs near King's Cross and enjoyed the cathartic experience of sharing their mutual hatred of senior management.

She was in a much better mood when she reached her flat and, preparing to spend the rest of the evening in, she poured a large glass of red wine and wandered round the flat looking at the Munch painting, the life drawing of Mike, and the things she had collected while living there. She had certainly enjoyed living here but she felt able to leave it because people mattered to her more than places. She decided to forego her Saturday morning run the next day to start sorting out the flat and then go to the studio in the hope of seeing Rebecca. The evening drifted into one of relaxation, watching the DVD of a French film and allowing herself more wine than usual for a lone evening. The wine plus the tensions of the week meant that she slept heavily and dreamt that she was wandering round an art gallery where her own paintings were on display: in her dream she was with someone male and attractive but, teasingly, she couldn't see the identity of the person.

Jenny's Mother

She was woken at 10.00 am by loud knocking on her door. It was Julian.

'This lady's been trying to raise you for some time but couldn't get an answer so I let her in.'

At first she couldn't work out who it was standing on the landing behind Julian. A woman in her mid-forties. Very smartly dressed for a Saturday morning in Camden. She took in the narrow designer jeans, soft leather ankle boots with heels and the leopard skin print jacket. Her hair was cut short and highlighted a brittle blonde; a dark lipstick had been painstakingly applied with a lipbrush.

Then realisation hit her. It was Jenny's mother. Once in the flat she began a diatribe.

'I've come to collect the rest of Jenny's things and I'd like you to pass a message on to your brother that Jenny doesn't want to see him or talk to him right now.'

Miranda knew that Toby would be devastated. Having dressed hastily in her jogging outfit and with uncombed hair and no make-up, Miranda felt at an extreme disadvantage with this well-dressed, heavily perfumed woman but she had to speak up for her brother.

'This is so unfair on Toby. What about the baby?'

'We'll take care of that. I'm quite capable of looking after my daughter and I can't see what Toby could contribute anyway. He certainly isn't in a position to make financial payments.'

Her anger only increased when Miranda allowed her into the spare room to look for Jenny's things.

'I can't imagine how they lived here; it's disgraceful. I'm surprised that you thought it was suitable to expect a young vulnerable woman to live in a place like this.'

'I'm not their landlord, Mrs Fitzgerald. Toby asked me if I would help them out and it was Jenny who asked if they could flat sit over the summer when I was away.'

'Of course she would. That's what he wanted her to do but you should see how distressed she's been; crying and sleeping all the time. You've both got a lot to answer for. I only hope this doesn't damage the baby.'

When she left Miranda was shaken by the attack. Totally unprepared for the onslaught she hadn't really offered any form of defence and she was furious at being the recipient of such an outpouring that, if anything, should have been directed at Toby.

She called Toby's mobile and when she got the answerphone left a message.

'Hi, it's Saturday at eleven and I'm angry. I've been verbally attacked by Jenny's mother. What a bitch. This has got nothing to do with me, Toby. It should be your problem.'

In contrast at the studio it was all calmness and as if this nasty event had never happened. A few of the others were there quietly working. Rebecca made coffee and Max hugged her and asked if she'd mind sitting for him for a while. It was pleasantly mindless sitting on the couch while Max drew: she was occupied without having to do anything and could let her mind drift.

Later she got back to the flat to find flowers propped against her door with a note attached.

Hi. Julian let me in. Sorry about fuss – she is a cow but I'll sort it and hopefully get out of your hair. Thanks for all your help. Really appreciated it. T xx

Now that she was calm she could smile. Typical of Toby's bravado and male charm. She doubted if he could charm Jenny's mother so easily but that was no longer her problem.

Chapter 14

Joel

The real problem came the next week in college. Malcolm emailed Miranda to request a meeting with her in the faculty office:

'There is an important matter we need to discuss urgently.'

Mysterious? Maybe there'd been a change of plan about the funding but then why only her? No one else seemed to have an email of that nature. Miranda had a slight feeling of trepidation; she hated being summoned in this way even if the curtness of the email was typical of Malcolm's style.

He wasn't alone in the office; Angela was there but positioned rather oddly in a chair slightly behind him with a notebook on her lap.

'Sit down, Miranda.'

Malcolm gestured to one of the low armchairs in front of the desk. Designed, she felt, to make you feel at a disadvantage in a formal meeting as he was sitting upright and protected by the desk in a position of authority.

'I'm afraid this is an unpleasant matter. There is a problem involving one of the students who was on your foundation course.'

'Yes. How can I help?'

Malcolm continued as if she hadn't spoken.

'In fact, his mother has been to see me with her concerns. Mrs Richardson; and she has made a serious complaint against you.'

'Mrs Richardson?' Miranda was bewildered. She couldn't think who this was.

'Joel Richardson.' Malcolm helpfully supplied. 'Does that help?'

It certainly did. Her mind was like a whirlwind.

'Joel? I don't understand. What is this about?'

'He has made, via his mother, an allegation of sexual harassment.'

'What! That's ridiculous.'

'That may be so but this is a very serious allegation and we have to investigate it. Mrs Richardson was in some distress when she came here. She said that Joel had been behaving oddly for some time and she finally managed to get him to tell her what was worrying him. Admittedly he is no longer a student at this college but he was when the alleged incidents took place.'

'What incidents?' She could hardly speak. 'What am I supposed to have done?'

'Made inappropriate advances, suggestive comments and even touching him.'

'No, that's not what happened. That's what he did to me.'

There, it was out and as soon as she'd said it she realised how feeble this sounded.

Malcolm and Angela both looked surprised.

'Did you report this?' Angela asked.

'Well, no I didn't.' And Miranda tried to explain her decision to keep it to herself to avoid the damage it would do to all concerned if she made a formal complaint.

'But Miranda,' Malcolm said. 'There are codes of conduct and procedures that should be applied in cases like this. We would expect you of all people to be aware of this.'

'Yes, yes, I know, but I preferred to handle it myself.'

'So you say, but I'm still not clear about your reason for concealing it.'

She didn't like the sound of the word 'concealing'; it suggested that she was being deceptive.

'I really thought it was an adolescent phase thing. I knew his father had died recently and didn't want to create any more trouble for the family.'

Angela intervened.

'If he made the sexual advances to you then surely you must have been upset.'

'Of course I was.'

'Yet you still didn't do anything about it.' Angela's voice was soft but the tone was full of implication.

Then it was Malcolm again. They were attacking her with questions and she was struggling to respond.

'You didn't report this officially but did you tell anyone else; a friend or colleague who could confirm what you're saying?'

She knew she had no control of the conversation and she was not defending herself successfully. But it was impossible to be calm and she raised her voice.

'No! I told you. I didn't want to create a bigger problem so I just didn't tell anyone.'

'Well, there certainly is a big problem now, Miranda.' Malcolm said. 'And there are other things. In addition to the episodes of inappropriate behaviour, Mrs Richardson also says that you encouraged him to draw portraits of you, one of which you then defaced in a strange way, and on one occasion when you returned some work to him he discovered that you had left your diary in his portfolio (presumably with the intention that he could read it); a diary which contained private details about your personal life.'

'No, that's wrong,' Miranda interrupted. 'He stole my diary so that he could find out what I was doing and then he brought it round to my flat.'

'So, he gave it to you and admitted stealing it?' Malcolm asked.

'No, he brought it when I was away on holiday and left it with my brother who was in the flat.'

'Does your brother know Joel?' Angela asked.

'No, but he mentioned that he thought he was weird and he'd seen him hanging around outside the house.'

'And surely at that stage you must have told your brother your concerns about Joel?' Angela again.

It was becoming more like a court of law every minute.

'No, I didn't say anything.'

There was a brief silence and then Malcolm continued.

'He was also concerned that you might have been stalking him.'

'How?' She was incredulous. This was getting worse each minute.

'Following him around. He said there were a number of occasions when you appeared in places when he was out with other students, in a coffee bar or somewhere.'

'Again that was what he was doing to me. He kept being in places where I was. I think he was outside the studio where I paint one evening, I saw him in Camden although he doesn't live there and he was hanging around one day in Russell Square when I was meeting a friend there.'

'And if you were with people on any of these occasions did you tell them that you suspected him of following you?'

'No.' By now she was hardly speaking, just shaking her head.

'Well, this doesn't look good,' Malcolm said. 'Unfortunately it's your word against his and he is a vulnerable young man whereas you were in a position of responsibility and had a duty of care.'

'But none of it is true.'

'Yes, but you've demonstrated that you have no way of supporting your version of the events.'

Now shock was being replaced by anger.

'It isn't a version. It's the truth. It's what actually happened.'

There was silence from Malcolm and Angela until she was forced to ask.

'What happens now?'

'I'll ask Mrs Richardson to come in to see me again,' Malcolm said, 'and I will tell her what you've told me, though no doubt she will wonder why you didn't report any of this. And we'll take it from there, but I do suggest that you get some legal advice.'

Miranda was deeply shocked. Her mind flew back to the thoughts she had had about how she needed to protect Joel and his family: and then to her initially confident decision that she could handle the problem herself. How could she have been so naive? And by adopting this passive response she had left herself vulnerable and open to this counter-accusation.

But what she found hardest to accept was the reaction of Malcolm and Angela. Although she wouldn't have expected deep sympathy, Miranda had hoped for some measure of support from professional colleagues. She was horrified by their cold, distant attitude. They made her feel like a stranger. She had a sickening fear and dread of the possible consequences and she could feel her life dissolving around her.

She had tried to protect Joel and his family and now what had happened was being used to destroy her career. She went over all the evidence and accepted that there was no way she could prove any of this. She had never felt so lonely.

She had to tell someone, and it needed to be someone who understood the college situation from the inside. Susannah was the obvious choice: calm, rational Susannah.

As usual Susannah was the best person to ask for advice that really worked. She didn't become emotional and empathetic as Anni would have done but simply assessed the situation objectively and came up with a practical response. She possessed a kind of transatlantic pragmatism that Miranda found reassuring. She listened to all Miranda had to say before making any comment.

'OK, you took a decision and maybe it wasn't the best one but it was what you saw as right at the time. So don't beat yourself up over it: now we have to sort it out.'

'The we is reassuring,' Miranda said. 'I'm so mad at myself that I didn't discuss this with you to start with but I really would appreciate your support now.'

Susannah as usual was organised and already planning.

'The first thing is to get legal advice. Try union representation to see what help they can offer before you decide about employing a professional lawyer. Remember that could be costly. Meanwhile, I'll do a bit of quiet sniffing around about Joel to find out more about him, see what he's been like with other tutors and students. You never know what we might turn up. If he's done anything like this previously then it would be useful evidence to use in your defence.'

'I'm deeply grateful for your help,' Miranda said. 'And for the moment I'd like to keep it between the two of us.'

'Of course,' Susannah agreed.

Miranda felt in a kind of limbo. She entered into a particularly solitary phase and she was aware of her emotions being reflected in her artwork. She was following her urge to use dark palettes. She called these her mood drawings, where she tried to achieve subtle effects by working without obvious colour. She experimented with palettes of ebony, coal, sable and pitch. She was aiming for a sort of tactile darkness and the creation of tenebrous shades. She worked in very close contact with the drawings, using her fingers to blur the shading to achieve a velvety sheen, and incorporating chalk and wax to highlight certain areas.

It was oddly satisfying to be alone now; Toby called her only occasionally, her friends and work colleagues were engaged in their own activities and the studio group had not resumed regular sessions. She missed Mike and there had been no one to replace him; any relationship would seem insubstantial and mundane after him. There had been a few invitations to social events which she had turned down with the excuse of work, and her previously frequent meetings with Anni had ceased now that she was totally absorbed in her new life with Pete.

She tried to push the Joel case to the back of her mind but it was constantly lurking there, waiting to emerge. She had consulted legal representatives at the union and had been offered support in any interviews with the faculty heads and/or Mrs Richardson. The opinion was that Joel's case was slight: he wasn't citing an actual assault but some vague accusations of harassment and pursuit. The fact that he was no longer a student at college and that he had not apparently discussed this with anyone at the time was also in her favour. It was suggested that she write up a dossier of all the occasions when his behaviour towards her had been suspicious or evidence of harassment and this could be used to argue the case that he was motivated by revenge because she had rejected his initial advances.

As a distraction she had developed a new fascination with climbing and had watched documentary programmes, read newspaper articles and watched any news items about climbing, trying to imagine the experiences of Mike and his fellow climbers.

She spent some time researching the area in Patagonia where they had gone to climb, in a desire to get closer to their experiences. She found out that El Chalten meant 'smoking mountain' and was built in 1985 to secure a disputed border with Chile. A virtual tour showed her a collection of low (mainly wooden) buildings scattered over rather uninteresting grassland and a tiny white town church. Some of the hostels resembled the sort of structures you saw in Alpine villages but without all the 'Sound of Music' window boxes and colour. But when the view swung to the mountains it took her breath away. The sheer scale of the snow covered peaks and the glittering glaciers made it magical.

She called into the travel bookshop in Covent Garden one evening to look for some reading material. There were so many accounts of expeditions that it was proving confusing and then she noticed Joe Simpson's 'Touching the Void'. She had seen the film with Mike and had found it intensely beautifully photographed and scary in terms of the accident. A book that she had recently read a review of was 'No Way Down: Life and Death on K2'.

Happy with her purchases she left the store and decided to walk back to Euston to pick up a bus to Camden. Crossing over High Holborn she met Jude. What a transformation. The sulky and rebellious student was eager to tell her that she had been accepted at Central St Martin's and was studying Fashion. She had projects she would like to discuss with Miranda and work to show her so they arranged a date for coffee.

Chapter 15

Jude

They met in Caffe Vergnano in New Street Square, Holborn, which was convenient for both of them. Miranda particularly liked this coffee chain with its tiny black coffee cups and saucers, and red and black decor. The coffee, which was made in a traditional Italian espresso machine, was strong and intense, served automatically with glasses of water. On her first visit the barrista carefully explained that you needed to sip water before each drink of espresso to get a kick every time.

Jude's hair had been cut short, slicked back and dyed blonde; she was dressed in a short skirt in a tartan fabric with black lace patterned tights and a faux fur trimmed gilet over a camisole: a crazily eclectic style that suited her. She had brought her sketchbook to show Miranda and gabbled enthusiastically about her designs and how valuable she found the course. She was clearly living life close to the edge and talked in a frenzied way, flitting from one topic to another. Jude didn't so much drink her coffee as play with it, filling the tiny cup with three sachets of sugar, stirring it repeatedly, lifting it up and then putting it down again without drinking it. She answered her mobile and responded to text messages several times, which interrupted any real attempt at sustained conversation.

Miranda sipped her own coffee thoughtfully, enjoying the adrenalin rush while considering that Jude was clearly getting her high from a stronger source. Jude was animated and excited about her work but was also agitated and hyperactive, talking fast, constantly switching topics, asking Miranda questions and not waiting for the answers. Classic signs of cocaine use, Miranda thought. As a student herself Miranda had flirted with cannabis and, occasionally, amphetamines, but had not progressed to regular social drug taking. However, she had come to recognise the signs of drug use in the young people that she worked with.

But, whatever the stimulus, Jude's sketchbook showed real inspiration; she had made it into a type of journal with descriptive text and even short diary entries about where she had gained her inspiration and sourced her materials. Miranda could see her own influence here as she had encouraged her students to see the value of recording things in their working notebooks. Like writers, she felt that artists needed to document the evidence.

What was really impressive, however, was that Jude had secured herself a trip to New York to visit some fashion houses and to attempt to make contacts to find work. Miranda was delighted to see what Jude had achieved and felt vindicated in her support of Jude against Angela. She had to admit to herself that she even felt professionally envious of how much experience this young girl had gained. The New York visit was truly exciting.

They had been so absorbed that Miranda had barely noticed the other occupants of the coffee bar, non-other than Gabrielo, the charming Italian barrista. Her eyes were drawn to a couple sitting at a table near the window and, with a slightly sickening feeling, she realised that it was Joel; but unusually, he was with a girl. She had never seen Joel alone with a girl, so maybe that was good news. The girl was wearing blue jeans and a padded jacket, with short fair hair and no make-up. She didn't look English but had that pale, washed out poverty stricken look of so many young Eastern Europeans.

As if he knew she was observing him, Joel looked up and they made eye contact. He stared boldly without acknowledging her and without any indication of recognition. She casually observed to Jude that Joel was sitting by the window.

'Do you know who the girl is? Don't recognise her as one of our students.'

Jude looked in their direction with little interest.

'Oh, yeah, it's the creep, Joel. She wasn't at college; think she might be an au pair or a language student. Polish or something.'

Well, if she was a girlfriend that was promising and should mean that Joel would leave her and his adolescent fantasies alone. She watched Joel lean over the table to take the girl's hand and kiss her; it made her feel slightly nauseous.

'Jude, what would you say if I told you he's accused me of sexual harassment?'

Jude's reaction was to burst out laughing.

'What! In his dreams. He's a total fantasist.'

'It's serious, Jude. His mother has made an official complaint and Malcolm and Angela are investigating.'

'And no doubt the Prince of Darkness and his sidekick are getting an illicit thrill out of all.'

'Joel is a number one creep and all the students know that. Tell you what, I'll go and see the Prince myself and give him the lowdown on Joel.'

'That's good of you, Jude, but maybe we should wait to see what happens next.'

Miranda felt that Jude was possibly not the best person to act as her advocate with the faculty heads, given her previous history with them. But Jude's reaction was worth a lot in restoring her self esteem.

Now the immediate problem was to avoid any direct contact with Joel here in the coffee bar and she hoped they would leave soon. She left Jude at the table while she went to the back of the shop to find the toilets. When she got back Jude had left the table with sketchbooks and notepads spread out on it, and was outside on the street smoking. Trust Jude to leave everything so casually, but at least Joel and the girl had gone. Miranda collected the books and papers together and looked for the bill. That was when she discovered one of the paper napkins with a drawing of a heart and what seemed to be a dagger slicing through it and the name Miranda scrawled beneath. Hardly the sort of thing Jude would leave for her so it looked as if Joel was still determined to find tiny ways to torment her. She shoved it into her bag to keep for evidence but in the knowledge that it would probably be useless as she might be accused of drawing it herself.

The meeting with Jude had been stimulating and, after conversations with other artists, Miranda usually felt renewed vigour for her own work. Jude was eager that they should meet again and suggested that Miranda visit her. She was living in a shared house with a few other 'arty' types and they were using part of the house to showcase some of their work.

As Miranda walked home she considered the implications of the unexpected meeting with Joel.

When she was talking to Jude she had temporarily forgotten the problem until he appeared in the cafe as if to haunt her. Any respite from thinking about Joel's accusation was always short-lived: it was a constant, underlying nagging concern that affected everything she did. And the worst thing was that Malcolm and Angela had made her feel guilty. She was the victim but because of their lack of support she had been portrayed as the guilty one, leaving Joel free to enjoy taunting her (if he was enjoying what he was doing).

She now understood how it was possible for an innocent person to be accused of a crime they had not committed and not be able to defend themselves. It was very scaring.

Susannah was being a great help but at college Miranda was finding it hard to concentrate on her work and to behave as normal. She was reluctant to get too close to her new students and was not able to develop the friendly rapport which she usually tried to establish at the start of a new term. As far as she knew her colleagues other than Susannah were not aware of what she was going through but there had been a few observations that she didn't look well and Jasmin had expressed concern that her mood seemed to be low.

Too late she acknowledged that she should have acted by at least confiding in someone after Joel's first approach. It had been a relief to tell Jude, to get her reaction and to find out what the other students thought of Joel. But none of this helped in putting forward her case, or, what Malcolm insisted on calling, her 'version' of the events.

The Squat

Jude lived in Balham, South London, with some people she described as an informal Arts Group. She wanted Miranda to see their work and suggested she come over one weekend evening.

What she hadn't told Miranda was that they lived in a squat. It was in the centre of a Georgian terrace, a house that had once been opulent but since being unoccupied was showing signs of neglect. The front door was padlocked which suggested there was no one at home. Jude had never been bothered about time-keeping so it was no surprise that she apparently wasn't there. Miranda walked round to the back of the house to find a fairly large untended garden with overgrown shrubs and broken statuary. Some of the windows in the basement and ground floor were boarded up but looked relatively intact on the upper stories, with pieces of fabric draped over some of them.

She couldn't find a back entrance so went round to the front where she saw Jude walking down the road with another girl and a guy, all carrying an assortment of plastic carrier bags.

Jude produced a key to the padlock and opened the door on to a large, empty hallway that was pooled in shadows. A wide, uncarpeted staircase wound up into the darkness above.

'We live upstairs,' Jude explained.

The rooms were virtually empty of furniture apart from an old sofa and a few chairs. Jude showed her round the rooms, which were mainly painted in white. There seemed to be an uncountable number of people there; mattresses, sleeping bags and boxes of personal belongings in two rooms indicated haphazard sleeping arrangements and one room was dedicated to communal living with a Butler sink and gas hob. There was no sign of a fridge.

'How do you live here?' Miranda asked. 'What about facilities and stuff?'

'Oh, we've had the water and gas reconnected and we get by with candles and oil lamps for lighting.'

'But what about the legal side of things? Aren't you afraid of being turned out or arrested?'

'You don't get arrested for squatting,' Jude patiently explained. 'Anyway, we're doing the community a favour. Do you know there are about seven hundred thousand empty houses in England and so many homeless people? This place was a wreck when we moved in. We painted a bit, mended some of the windows and cleared a pile of junk out of the yard. The only way they can get us out is by gaining entry when we're not here and we try to leave someone in all the time.'

'Well, there was no one here when I arrived and I would have had time to break in, if I'd been so inclined.'

'Yeah, well, if that happens we move on and find another one.'

More people had gathered in the communal room now, although it was unclear where they had come from. Jude and the guy she had come in with began unloading the carrier bags on to a bench.

'In your honour, Miranda, we're going to eat together tonight.'

A curious assortment of food was being produced from the bags. It seemed to consist mainly of sandwiches in triangular plastic containers from chains like 'Eat' and 'Pret a Manger', a couple of loaves of Sainsbury's bread, some tins, some battered cans of beer and a couple of bottles of red wine.

'Must be a pretty expensive way to eat,' Miranda commented.

'We don't buy it.'

'You mean you steal it?' She certainly didn't feel like eating stolen food.

'God, no, we're Freegans.'

'Oh, I get it. You look in skips outside supermarkets?'

'Basically, yes. You have no idea how much stuff gets thrown away because it's near a sell by date or a bit disfigured: it's one of the major crimes of capitalist society.'

'All you have to do is know the times of day the shops do their chuck out and wait to get into the skips. In fact, some of the guys in the coffee chains are good sorts and tip us the wink when they're ready to clear out.'

'And the alcohol; was that thrown away?'

'No, Adam here is our expert wine shopper,' indicating the small dark haired guy who'd arrived with her. 'He liberates it from supermarkets where they're not too observant. But never from privately owned or ethnic corner stores.'

So there was a distinct moral code for this way of living.

The freegan food and liberated wine was surprisingly good and Miranda found herself admiring the young people for their alternative lifestyle. Jude showed her the upper floor where artwork was displayed, ranging from sculpture made from found items, huge paint splattered abstract canvases and mixed media pieces.

'We sometimes do performance art in here as well. You know, we meet other people who join us like students studying theatre and music. There's just too much commercial art out there and our idea is to get together with people who aren't restricted by movements.'

Back in her flat that night Miranda was relieved to return to home comforts but found herself considering her own situation. College was a definite problem with this issue of Joel and the antagonism of Malcolm and Angela: she had no real need to stay in Camden or even in London. There was no relationship to keep her here. There were positives in her life, like Kate and Paul's interest in her work and the group she met at Rebecca's studio, who often had contacts in the art world.

Money was an obvious issue but she could, she thought, live in a more economical way without actually going down Jude's route of squatting and freegan living.

Chapter 16

The College

It didn't take long for things to happen. At the beginning of the next week Malcolm called Miranda to a meeting as soon as she arrived at the college. She asked for more notice so that she could arrange union representation. It was arranged for later in the week, giving Miranda time to meet her representative and plan their strategy. She understood that Mrs Richardson and Joel would both be present. She handed over the dossier that she had compiled and chose suitably smart, professional clothes for the meeting. Andy, the legal representative was calm and reassuring.

'You've no idea how many of these kinds of cases we see.'

'And how are they usually resolved?'

'They're all different but given the age of your student and the vagueness of his accusations I feel confident.'

Susannah had provided some anecdotal accounts of Joel's 'creepy' behaviour. The tutors generally regarded him with indifference, except for noting that he was uncommunicative and lacked social skills, but the students she had spoken to had been more forthright in their assessment, which in every case was unflattering. He seemed to be an object of either ridicule or pity.

When Miranda and Andy entered the faculty office, Mrs Richardson was already there but Joel was not. Introductions were made and Malcolm began. What he had to say came as a surprise.

'Joel has decided not to be present. Mrs Richardson came on her own today to say that they won't be pursuing the matter any further.'

So that was it. Mrs Richardson didn't say anything.

'We need to be clear about this,' Andy said. 'Is it correct that the allegations are being withdrawn?'

A terse 'yes', from Malcolm.

'In that case I need a few minutes with Miranda.'

They went outside into the corridor.

'You can see what's happened,' Andy said. 'He knows he's taken it too far and now he's bottled out but this is your opportunity to cite your case; that is, that he was pursuing you and this false accusation has caused you unnecessary stress. So you can claim compensation.'

She didn't need time to decide.

'I don't want to do it. I just want to try to forget it.'

'Think carefully about this, Miranda,' Andy said. 'He has completely upset your life and caused you grief at your work place by allowing his fantasies to run riot. I don't feel that the management of this college have handled the situation well, and they need to be shown that they have to offer more support to their tutors. You acted on instinct the first time and ended up in a situation where it was difficult to defend yourself. Now you have the opportunity to see that justice is done.'

'But what would I achieve? My relationship with college is already damaged. My original reason for not reporting Joel was his family circumstances and they haven't changed: I didn't want to cause his mother any more stress after the death of her husband. Joel is a very dysfunctional guy with personality problems and if I insist on pursuing this it will only damage his future.'

'Well, I think you're very forgiving, Miranda. Not many people would be willing to do that.'

'I do have a more selfish reason which is, that if I now make a formal complaint about Joel it will become public and I'll be a focal point for gossip. I don't think I could stand that. I just want to leave the whole nasty business behind me.'

They returned to the room and, after Andy had explained that Miranda did not wish to pursue a counter-accusation against Joel, Mrs Richardson left, still without any comment. It was as if she was pretending that Miranda was not there.

'What actually happened?' Miranda asked Malcolm.

'Nothing, in fact. She came to the meeting today and said immediately that they were withdrawing their complaint and that you would hear no more about it.'

'And the reason?' Andy asked.

'She didn't give one.'

'Was there an apology?' Miranda asked.

'No, as I told you, that's all she said.'

It certainly wasn't worth pointing out to Malcolm the needless anxiety and stress that this had created for her; she knew that sympathy would not be forthcoming from that quarter but even so she was unprepared for his comment as they were preparing to leave.

'We are all very pleased this has ended so easily, but I suggest, Miranda, that in future you are more circumspect in the relationships you establish with your students. We don't want a repetition of this unpleasant business.'

Andy was furious and wanted her to reconsider her decision not to place a counter-accusation.

'How can you bear to work with that man?' He asked when she still refused.

'Maybe I won't have to for much longer,' she said.

Chapter 17

The Yoga Room

It was an autumn evening after college and Miranda was in Vikram's yoga room. Vikram was about to leave for India for several months; his intention being to study the philosophical and spiritual aspects of yoga. He was taking an extended break from his career job as a senior stylist in an up-market hairdressing salon in Mayfair. During one of the occasional discussions he had with the group he explained that he was becoming less enthusiastic about his career because of the increasing commercialisation of the organisation he worked for. He had reached the stage, he said, where yoga was a big part of his life and he wanted an opportunity to devote an intense period of time to it.

As a farewell to the people who regularly attended the yoga room, he had invited them to join him for a candlelit meditation.

They sat in a circle, a lighted candle in front of each yoga mat and perfumed oil with resonances of frankincense and sandalwood burning subtly. They began with chanting. Vikram led the chant, producing a soft, mellifluous OUM sound which gathered in volume and depth until it echoed and re-echoed around the room. Sitting cross-legged, with eyes closed and fingertips resting lightly on knees, all there was to concentrate on was the ever growing and deepening rhythmic sound. The echoes and reverberations took on a musical quality. Then the chanting died away and was replaced by a warm silence. At first they opened their eyes and focused on the candle flame then at some point that seemed appropriate each person closed their eyes and concentrated on their own vision.

Miranda could see the flickering shape of the candle flame through closed eyelids. Then the flame began to lengthen and extend as the area around it deepened in colour. Shades of purples and greens floated across her retina, swirling and dissolving. Then it all seemed to settle into a more static soft darkness. But something was emerging out of the darkness, growing distinctly larger and nearer; and then she could see it, almost felt she could reach out and touch it. It was a tiny, coiled gold serpent lying on a bed of indigo velvet.

For a few seconds the image completely filled her mind and the external world was shut out.

Gradually noises began to intrude; there was some gentle shuffling and the voice of Vikram asking everyone to take their time opening their eyes to become accustomed once more to their material surroundings. Miranda was reluctant to relinquish this image but knew it would have to go. Vikram invited a brief discussion of shared experiences for those who wanted to and she listened to accounts of images seen, or the lack of them. She didn't feel ready to share hers publically but when the others had left she described to Vikram what she had seen.

'Vikram, I had a beautiful image – a tiny gold serpent lying on a bed of indigo velvet. It was like something you might have seen in an Ancient Egyptian tomb.'

'That, Miranda, is something to envy.'

'Why, does it have a meaning?'

'Yes, it's Kundalini; that's the energy that lies dormant at the base of the spine. There are two circular branches which encircle the chakras and this energy charges and activates them. It is a rare experience.'

'So, why do you think it happened to me?'

'It means that your mind is operating on a higher, more spiritual dimension. In fact, you may have been very close to an out of body experience.'

'It certainly felt strangely beautiful. I think I have you to thank for creating the right atmosphere.'

'Go carefully when you leave Miranda. You have been in a state of heightened consciousness and you need to ease yourself back into that noisy world out there.'

It was true that as she left Vikram's house and walked towards King's Cross she did have the sensation that she wasn't quite part of the people thronging around her. She descended the steps into the underground, automatically collecting a free copy of the Evening Standard from one of the young men outside the station. The tube ride was a gentle blur and, emerging from the station in Camden Town, she considered her options. She didn't feel like going straight to the flat; there was no one there now that Toby had finally moved his things out and she had invited Anni and Pete to join her for supper later in the evening so a short spell in a coffee shop would be a good transition. Cafe Nero seemed the best option, with its comfy leather chairs and background classical music to reflect her mood. The one on Camden High Street was unusually quiet so she secured herself a chair near the window and sipped her coffee thoughtfully. She was vaguely aware of a few people sitting at the other tables and then, remembering the newspaper she casually flicked through it.

The article was on one of the inside pages, only a column but the headline was clear enough.

British climber killed in Patagonia

Mesmerised, she began to read.

A British climber has died in Patagonia on an expedition to climb the North Pillar of Mount Fitzroy.

He has been named as Mike Matthews from Glasgow. The other two members of the team were Duncan Crawford, also from Scotland and Tom Kennedy, an Australian. The climbers had successfully reached the summit and were making their descent when they encountered a snow storm followed by an ice fall.

Details of the events are not yet clear but it would seem that the two surviving climbers had to abandon their attempts to rescue Matthews when the storm worsened. Weather conditions also made it impossible for a rescue team to set out.

That was it. Frantically she searched through the rest of the paper to see if there were any 'further details' but that sort of report would not be worth a longer article, nor was it likely to feature on any radio or television news items. She mechanically drank her coffee and gazed around the room, as if looking for help. But from where? No one here knew that in those few moments her life had changed. It was impossible to believe that Mike, that vibrant, energetic man no longer existed. The realisation that now she could never see him again was hard to accept.

Leaving the coffee shop she drifted into a supermarket and began mindlessly throwing items into her trolley for the evening ahead. What was she doing? Why was she doing such a mundane thing as buying food when Mike was dead? Surely she should be contacting people, finding out what had happened.

Would there be a memorial service? She knew enough about climbing to realise that a funeral would no doubt be out of the question. And then it hit her: she knew almost nothing about him. She didn't have his home address or any information about his family. He had never talked about his family circumstances or the past, unless it related to climbing. And, if she didn't know anything about them, why should his family know about her? It didn't even seem that she would be given the opportunity to mourn him properly.

Numbed of emotion now she made her purchases and left the store. Passing the flower stall she felt she should buy flowers. There were white and yellow freesias. A flower that she loved and that occasionally Mike had bought for her.

Hampstead

People who knew about Mike were kind to her but she was in a strange vacuum where she wanted to grieve but couldn't do so in any public, legitimate way as her relationship with Mike had not been established enough. If she had been a wife or fiancé or had even been close to his family there would have been acceptable ways for her to express her feelings but as it was she knew almost nothing about him before they had met. It was conceivable that she was not his only girlfriend, in fact it was possible that he was actually married. Shortly after the news of his death she googled his name and came up with details about his climbing experiences and achievements but very little about his personal life. As she trawled through climbing books and magazines she checked indexes for mention of his name and it did occur several times but only as a brief reference; he wasn't enough of a celebrity to be featured prominently. He had left her so abruptly in Lisbon that they didn't even have future plans; she had hoped he would come back to her but, on reflection, she acknowledged that she had no evidence for thinking that, only her own desire.

'You're looking stressed out, Miranda,' Susannah had said at college. 'How about joining us for brunch on Sunday? We can walk on the heath after and have a good chat; there's never any time here.'

'Yeah, that sounds good.'

And Miranda realised that she was actually looking forward to something.

Susannah lived in Hampstead Village in a superbly renovated three storey Victorian townhouse with oriel and bay windows and a fanlight over the front door which was painted in a period colour of dark navy.

Miranda loved the way they lived. The whole of the ground floor was given over to a light and airy dining and family living area with French doors opening on to a flagstone patio. Upstairs were the study and the more formal living room which Miranda had seen when she had been invited to drinks parties in the evening. Sunday brunch was a bit of a ritual with Susannah's family; one of the few times in the week, she said, when she could make them all sit together. Bruce was a good-looking nine year old with masses of tangled curly dark hair and mischievous eyes. He talked, or rather shouted, volubly most of the time and had to be discouraged from racing around the room at terrifying speed. Edie was a pretty, disconsolate twelve year old who was only animated in the company of her peers. If forced to spend time with adults she retreated into her iPod or mobile phone, sending out clear signals that she did not intend to enter voluntarily into any form of communication. Miranda respected Edie's wishes and, after greeting her, took care not to break into her private world. Connie, however, was adorable. At six years old she was still enthusiastic about life and school and the world around her. She had inherited Susannah's artistic talents and spent ages on drawings and collages: she was allowed to sit at one end of the table so that she could spread out her paper and coloured crayons and draw while waiting for the food.

They ate eggs, cheese, cold meat and fruit served on generous platters. Susannah's husband, William, had the task of going to a nearby bakery for French loaves that were still warm from the oven. Susannah made huge cafetières of coffee and William prepared freshly squeezed orange juice. The Czech au pair joined them as she did for all meals. Susannah had once confided in Miranda that she was the most difficult au pair they had employed. Apparently she was homesick and had gone home for a long weekend only two weeks after starting work with them. Her parents had already been to the UK to visit her and Susannah had felt obliged to offer them a spare bedroom.

'I employed the girl to help me run the house and now I'm entertaining her family.'

Marika also spent hours phoning home on the landline or waiting for her parents to call. What they talked about Susannah had no idea because, even given the fact that it was in a foreign language, Marika's contribution to the conversation seemed to be limited to monosyllabic murmurings.

Susannah believed in providing good wholesome food even if they weren't able to all eat together regularly. A box of organic vegetables was delivered each week and when she could she shopped at Farmers' Markets at the weekend. But this girl refused to eat any fruit, vegetables or meat other than burgers and existed on a diet of cheese, bread and coke.

So this was the one meal of the week when she was somewhere in tune with the rest of the family.

After brunch they walked on the Heath, leaving Edie at home to commune with her friends on her mobile. It was one of those beautifully autumnal days when the colours of the leaves and trees were of infinite varieties of russets and browns. There was a fairly bracing wind which Bruce loved as he tore around manically.

'This is what I like about living in England,' Susannah said. 'The marked changes in the seasons; and autumn is most definitely the season when it really stars.' As they walked conversation naturally turned to college and the impending cuts. It was Susannah who introduced the topic.

'What are your thoughts on it Miranda?'

'I feel like I'm at a halfway house; everything's changing. Don't think I can take the atmosphere at college in the long term and I'm sure that Malcolm and Angela will not be moving on in the near future.'

Susannah agreed. 'Let's face it, where is there for them to go? They are intent on controlling everything and they have no insight because they can't see how damaging they are. Angela's interpersonal skills are zilch; I reckon she needs a course in anger management.'

'So, what are you going to do?' Miranda asked. 'Stay there or look for something else?'

'Well, I guess I'll hang around for a bit. I could do with the salary now while the kids are growing up so that I can employ people but William is doing OK so, even if my hours aren't cut I wouldn't mind reducing my teaching load. No doubt the financial aspect is different for you.'

'It is; it'll be hard to maintain my present lifestyle with a reduced pay cheque; there's plenty I could cut back on but just existing in London is expensive. And then, you know, things have changed because of Mike and this dreadful Joel episode and everything. To be honest, Susannah, I feel I've reached a bit of a watershed.'

Susannah was sensitive to her mood and suggested going to the cafe to talk.

'Let's dump the others; William can take them home later. Then we can talk in peace.'

They sat on the cafe terrace, wrapped up in coats and scarves with cups of coffee.

'What would you do, in my situation?' Miranda asked.

'I think you need to take a step back and get the big picture. We have been a bit worried about you at college recently. You've been edgy and, I don't know, ill at ease. Maybe, for example, you should put your MA on hold for a while; you could be getting over involved with fairly depressing stuff. It could get unhealthy.'

Miranda did have to admit that such an intense study of an artist like Munch had meant that some of his melancholia was seeping into her perspective on life.

'OK, I can see your point. I'm sure my supervisor would agree to a break; I don't have to finish it this year. And there is something else; it's about Anni. I would have said that Anni was my best friend; for a long time I thought she was a very good friend but after I met Mike I saw a different side to her. I realised that she was always there, coming to the flat, staying the night, offering to help with things, borrowing my clothes: it sounds ridiculous but I began to suspect that she was taking over my life; or was it a way of taking Mike from me?'

'I know that you had said something to her about her friendship with Mike, because she told me and she was totally unembarrassed about it.'

Susannah was measured in her reply. 'Yes, I did try to talk to her because I was concerned that she might be making you unhappy.'

'And, what did you think she was trying to do.'

'Anni can be a very seductive person but in truth I think she's actually rather shallow and she probably envied you Mike, your career and your circle of friends, as her life had been disrupted.'

'And now it's like our friendship never happened. She's completely absorbed in her new life with Pete, polite enough when I see her occasionally, like when they call into the wine bar; I think she only does that to show him off.'

'Exactly, so she's not much of a friend now that she's got what she wants.'

'And you're right, I have been edgy as you put it; feel haunted by things that have happened recently and the main problem I'm sure is college. I used to love it but now I can't relax there; I'm living in fear of being pounced on by Angela or Malcolm. It's stifling my own creativity as well as what I can do for my students.'

'Then give it up. Do what you want to do. Concentrate on your own work. It's beginning to sell and you've got the website so you don't even need to stay here. You could travel if you wanted to, for example.'

'You are so right. I do think that I need to get out of London for a while. I sometimes think back to the time I spent in Lisbon and wonder if I could enjoy working in that environment. The pace is so different and there's something appealingly quirky about that city.'

'Well, do it, Miranda. Just go.'

It was like an epiphany: an overwhelming relief. Of course, Miranda knew that the decision would be the easy part: the more difficult bit was putting it in practice. It would take courage but was undoubtedly achievable.

On the bus from Hampstead to Camden she worked it out. If she went to Lisbon it should be easy to live simply there once she had found somewhere inexpensive to live. Her daily needs should be economical and she could work undisturbed in the way she wanted to with complete freedom. Absorbed in thought, she almost missed her stop. Camden High Street was a typically crowded late Sunday afternoon and there were a number of people waiting to get both on and off the bus. Good manners seemed to break down as people pushed their way on and off simultaneously. Someone nudged her and made close physical contact with her as she got off; turning her head to see who it was there was a flicker of recognition before she realised that it was Joel. Then he was lost in the crowd on the pavement. She couldn't tell whether he had been getting on or off the bus. Either way, what was he doing here? She tried to be rational and tell herself that it was perfectly natural for any young person to be out at Camden Lock on a Sunday afternoon. But for most young people that tended to be a sociable occasion and she hadn't noticed anyone with him. And as usual, apart from that one time in Caffe Vergnano, he was alone.

Going into the house she met Julian and impulsively asked him in for a drink as she didn't want to be on her own immediately. He was in a particularly cheerful mood and was happy to accept.

Once in the flat with drinks poured, she casually asked.

'Were you in earlier in the day?'

'Yeah, why?'

'Just wondered if anyone had called while I was out.'

'Were you expecting someone?'

'Not exactly, thought Toby might have dropped round.'

But Julian hadn't noticed anyone. That didn't mean that Joel hadn't been there but even if he had there wasn't much she could do about it now that she had rejected Andy's advice to make a formal accusation. She was convinced that even if he wasn't technically 'stalking' her that he definitely was hanging around; there were too many coincidences. And there were the other things: the stolen diary, the drawing of her, the napkin left for her in the coffee shop, the weird email and the strange items in the post that she was convinced had come from him. Who could she take this to as evidence? Virtually all of it could be given a rational explanation or dismissed as her imagination. Except of course the key evidence which was the way he had touched her. So, to get anyone to take her seriously she would need to reveal the explicit details, and that was not something she wanted to do.

Susannah was correct in saying that she had seemed absorbed and stressed. There were complications in her life with her career problems, love life or lack of it and changes in her friendship group, but what no one else was aware of apart from Susannah was the sinister presence of Joel.

Chapter 18

Tom

Most of the tutors on the foundation course had had their hours cut. Miranda's had been reduced to four days a week. Once she had adapted to the financial implications, she took advantage of the extra day to spend on her own work and to do more reading and visiting free gallery exhibitions. It was pleasantly restful to have this extra time but it did make surviving financially in London increasingly difficult. One afternoon she allowed herself the treat of a visit to a Munch exhibition at Tate Modern. It was a unique opportunity to actually see his paintings and as the gallery was unexpectedly quiet she was able to spend time studying the canvases, drawn into them by the vibrancy of the colours and the pulsating emotions that emanated from them. There were several interpretations of 'The Vampire/Kiss' which she dwelt on before moving through the rest of the rooms.

Feeling re-energised about returning to her MA studies, she walked back through Covent Garden and Holborn and stopped off in Marchmont Street to browse in one of the second-hand bookstores where she occasionally found affordable Art books or paperback fiction. On her way to the station she passed the tiny, cheap cafe frequented by workmen and students who lived in the nearby halls of residence. The cafe was so small that all the eating area was on the outside terrace with a canopy cover. At this time of day the customers were primarily students who had no doubt surfaced late and were eating platefuls of pasta or bacon and eggs. She noticed one guy on his own sitting at a table with a half eaten plate of eggs and beans and mug of tea in front of him. He wasn't doing anything except staring at the table and fiddling with his mobile phone. Miranda had almost gone past when he looked up and met her eyes. It was Tom; almost unrecognisable but it was him. He looked wrecked: no longer the tanned, healthy, fit looking Antipodean that she remembered from Lisbon. When she approached him he looked vague.

'Hi, Tom: it is Tom? Do you remember me? We met in Lisbon; I was with Mike Matthews.'

'Oh, yeah, Miranda, hi. Sorry, I was miles away.'

'I know about Mike. At least, I read about it in the newspaper. What are you doing here?'

'Oh, just taking a bit of time out before I go home. I'm staying at the Generator round the corner so this is a good place to eat.'

He didn't seem interested in giving any other information, in fact, didn't seem to want to speak to her at all but she couldn't just walk away. This was her one opportunity to talk to one of the two people who had been with Mike and knew what had happened. How could he sit there without acknowledging how they were linked by this tragedy?

'Look, can I talk to you about what happened: all I know is what I read in that one article?'

'Yeah, sure:' although she sensed a reluctance.

He made no move to ask if she wanted to sit down and anyway, it was cold on the terrace and noisy from passing pedestrian traffic.

'Well, would it be OK if we went somewhere warmer? Can I buy you a drink?'

They crossed the street to the Lord Russell and she suggested a quiet table near the back of the pub.

He didn't offer to buy the drinks and she was surprised when he responded to her offer with a request for lemonade. Where was the hardened lager drinker of the Lisbon cafes?

She ordered red wine for herself; not the temperature or the mood for ice cold white wine spritzers.

It tasted acidic.

'God, tastes like something died in this.'

'What?' Tom looked up vacantly from his trance-like staring at the table.

'Oh, nothing. Just the wine tastes pretty foul.'

She drank it anyway while he sat there moodily staring at his glass. Was he ever going to speak, she wondered? And why wouldn't he look at her? The only way was to force the pace.

'Tom, I really need you to tell me what happened, if you can. It was such a shock finding out about Mike in that way.'

He raised his head and looked at her properly for the first time.

'It was all my fault.'

'What do you mean?'

Tom hunched over the table with his hands clasped around his glass, although he made no effort to drink it.

And then it all poured out.

'I mean I caused the accident, Miranda. It happened because I was stupid and became a liability.'

'How can you say it was your fault: it was an accident, wasn't it?'

'Sure,' he said reluctantly, 'it was an accident, but not in the way you think. I'd been taking stuff for a while to get me through my fears of climbing. I loved the sport, I was addicted to the adrenalin but I was also addicted to the stuff that made me able to do it.'

He moved edgily on his chair and Miranda leant forward encouragingly.

'So, what were you taking?'

'If I was preparing for a climb I'd take various things, amphetamines, speed and stuff mainly, and then once I was climbing I might need something else so I'd take along a few Valium and I carried a small flask with some scotch in it.'

'Why did you feel you needed to do this?' Miranda asked.

'It became part of my climbing routine. I couldn't stop climbing but I couldn't do it without the help. And when I wasn't climbing I was drinking heavily. I've always been in good shape and pretty fit so for a while I got away with it, although it was messing with my head. But this time it was a step too far.'

The tension in his voice increased as he said.

'I think Duncan suspected me even before we started that final ascent. We had been living in close proximity for a few days in El Chalten and I'm sure now that he noticed something: I'd usually pop a few pills before our evening drinking sessions and I'd sometimes need to get up in the night when I couldn't sleep to grab a couple of sleeping tablets. For all I know, he could have been through my backpack when I wasn't in the room.'

Tom hesitated and Miranda found herself quietly prompting him.

'So, what happened?'

'Anyway, that day, the day of the ascent, I felt nervous.'

By now Miranda felt she was with them on the mountain as he described the horror of what had taken place.

'The weather reports were not of the best and we had spent some time assessing whether or not to attempt it. I could have backed out then but the problem was that I really wanted to do it; in fact I felt I had to do it. It wasn't until we were actually on the mountain that I realised the mistake I had made and that I should have admitted how I felt before we set off.'

He paused, as if imagining himself back there with the horror.

'Once the weather turned bad I began to lose concentration, started feeling panicky and out of control. I was so petrified I was going to lose it that when we stopped for a drink I took a couple of Valium. I think Duncan saw me do that. Then, when we were making the descent we spent a couple of hours sheltering on a portaledge, deciding whether to hole up for the night or push ahead through the snowstorm.'

His voice sounded dry and raspy and he took a drink of the lemonade before continuing.

'At least, I think it was a couple of hours but by then I'd lost all track of time and I wasn't saying much. We ate and drank hot drinks and it was then that Duncan saw me taking a nip from my flask. He gave me a strange look and said quietly "You need to be careful, Tom". Once the decision was made to continue the descent I was like a zombie, following Mike but not thinking about what I was doing. I'd lost all connection with my surroundings and it just seemed to be me and what was going on in my head.'

Miranda could see that he was physically struggling now as he recalled the events. He kept twisting the glass in his hands and he moved his gaze to avoid eye contact with Miranda so that he seemed to be transfixed by something on the wall behind her head.

'Then I fell and I didn't want to get up. The snow seemed comforting and I just wanted to lie there. I knew that I couldn't do that and that I would freeze to death in no time but I actually didn't care. When the tension on the rope changed Mike must have known something was wrong. I don't think he could have actually seen me through the snow blizzard but he started to climb back up to help. I was vaguely aware of his voice which seemed to be miles away and maybe I saw him but my memories are all clouded. My first clear recollection was Duncan telling me I had to get up and then the discovery that Mike had gone. Don't know how we did the rest of the descent; I only got down because of Duncan. By the time we reached base camp we were both totally out of it and our first thought was to try to get a rescue started for Mike. But it was no good; the conditions meant that no one was able to attempt it.'

She could hear the increasing reluctance in his voice as he forced himself to continue with his confession.

'The next day in El Chalten Duncan challenged me about what I'd been doing. I admitted it all and I've never felt so bad in my life to see what that guy had gone through to save me when he'd lost a friend and a guy he really admired. Yeah, I felt like I was the lowest of the low. Duncan gave me a hard time about it but said he saw no point in spreading this around the climbing community as long as I agreed to his conditions.'

'His conditions?' For the first time Miranda felt able break into his monologue.

'Yeah, that I should seek counselling and totally detox, give up the pills and the alcohol and give him my word I would never climb again in that state. And that's what I'm doing now; I'm fixed up with a counsellor here in London and I'll stay at the Generator until I'm ready to go back to Oz.'

'What will you do?' Miranda asked.

'Dunno, but guess I'll find something. Maybe a life guard on a beach,' he said cynically.

It was difficult for her to know how to react. What she felt was sheer anger at his irresponsibility mingled with a sort of pity for him as he looked so destroyed, thin and haggard as he sat hunched over the table. Her compassionate side prompted her to offer some reassurance, as she would have done with one of her students, but she could hardly resort to the cliché of 'You mustn't blame yourself' when clearly he was to blame.

There was another awkward silence but then, as she shifted around in her seat, he seemed to remember her presence and said, almost apologetically

'How long had you been with Mike?'

'Oh, not even a year although it seemed much longer in some ways. I was ...' and she hesitated, not wanting to say 'in love with him' or express any of the other emotions that overtook her whenever she thought of him. So she let it tail off.

'He was pretty fixated on you, you know.'

'Was he?' Her eagerness for more was obvious and she felt herself blushing.

'Yeah, he talked about you a bit. You know, mainly when we'd all had a drink and were kind of randomly talking.'

'But he wasn't so fixated that he wanted to stay with me in Lisbon and finish the holiday we had started together. I was sure you'd persuaded him to leave.'

'No way; he suggested coming with me. Think he'd had enough of the cultural scene and he was keen to get in some serious exercise. I was just a ready excuse; he'd have probably done it anyway.'

'So, did he ever say he felt bad about leaving me there?'

'Not really, in fact I thought you guys had agreed it. He did say that he didn't like to be tied down and that he felt you were the clinging type.'

So, she was clinging? Miranda felt a flash of anger, although not sure whether it was at Mike for having said it or herself for presenting herself in that way. She had thought their relationship had been fulfilling and exciting; she had no real idea that he had felt that she was over-possessive. It was upsetting to see herself in that way. But what was the point; he was dead and couldn't be given the chance to explain himself?

Then it occurred to her to ask about Duncan.

'Well, once we'd had our heart to heart and I'd agreed to follow his action plan, he didn't speak to me again except for essential things like making the arrangements to go home and sorting out practicalities. We didn't even fly back to the UK together. Once we got to the airport for the flight to Heathrow he told me he'd changed his seat number and we wouldn't be sitting together. He told me not to look out for him at Heathrow but to make my own arrangements. He did say it would be OK with him if he never saw me again.'

'All I know is that he's gone to work as a guide in a mountaineering club in Switzerland. So, I guess he'll be taking tourists up the Alps. Anyway, if you want to read the sanitised version he's written an article about what happened, or rather a journalist who interviewed him has written it.'

'Oh, where can I find it?'

'It's in the Alpinist magazine, not sure which issue but you can find it online.'

Miranda was familiar with the publication as part of her obsessive research on climbing and had already bookmarked it on her laptop.

Once they were back out on Marchmont Street she wasn't sure how to part from him. She was reluctant to go and break this fragile link with Mike but she could hardly ask to meet him again and even if he agreed she could barely tolerate his misery. So they parted with platitudes from her 'Good luck and look after yourself', and a brief 'Yeah, bye' from Tom. She watched him walk down the street in front of her and turn the corner to make his way back to the Generator.

Once in the flat she logged on to her laptop and found Duncan's article.

Tragedy on Mount Fitzroy

Written by Ellie Foster after an interview with Duncan Crawford.

It's strange and weird to go back to that time and try to recapture how it was before the accident.

We were confident in our preparations and felt completely ready for the expedition. Weather had delayed us for several days in El Chalten where we'd taken the opportunity to chat to other climbers and do some networking. I'd climbed with Mike on several occasions before and we knew each other's tactics and felt comfortable together: if I had to be with anyone in a tricky situation I would have chosen Mike. He had immense grit and tenacity: he was a real hard-core climber, able to go without sleep for up to thirty hours and still be able to function clearly. Tom was the new member of our team but had a vast background of extreme sports and we reckoned we would be competent mentors.

The weather in Patagonia is volatile and you always know that there could be problems: every climber is aware that the only certainty in mountaineering is that there is no certainty.

So, we made our decision to go ahead based on all the information available: we did cover all the possibilities of adverse weather and unanimously wanted to seize the opportunity.

Initially it was brilliant. We set off in some warm sunshine and were treated to awesome views of the Fitzroy Tower and the unbelievably beautiful glaciers.

Then the wind began to pick up and visibility quickly lessened. The climb began to seem never-ending and it became an internal struggle. At no point did we consider aborting the ascent; in fact, we were pretty fixated on the idea of getting there and I think in truth we had begun to lose sight of anything other than our immediate goal. We reached the summit in a state of exhaustion and near delirium. Dark clouds had massed and we didn't have the visibility we had hoped for but there was still the overwhelming euphoria that claims you totally when you reach your goal. We celebrated with hot drinks and empanadas we had packed so many hours ago in El Chalten.

But on the descent we were increasingly aware of the potentially serious nature of our situation. Battling through snow storms and ever darkening clouds we took refuge for a few hours on a portaledge. Here we discussed whether to hole up there for the night or whether to continue. Regular checking of weather forecasts on our phones suggested that it was probably going to deteriorate. Sitting the night out then didn't seem such a good option if it meant battling on the next day through further storms with supplies nearly exhausted. We had more hot drinks and ate some chocolate before starting on the rest of the descent. We started off roped, with Mike leading and Tom between us two more experienced climbers. After a while it became clear that Tom was becoming disorientated, his progress was slowing and the conditions made it extremely difficult to communicate with him. Then he stopped without warning and slumped into the snow. The increased tension on the rope alerted Mike to the problem and he attempted to retrace his steps by climbing back up to Tom. But by now it was total whiteout; a further snow storm caught Mike in a vulnerable position and at that point he went over the edge into a crevasse. I was able to get down to Tom, who by this time was more aware of events around him. I debated the possibility of going down into the crevasse to rescue Mike but couldn't even see him let alone find a potentially safe route down. This is the moment dreaded by every climber; the decision to abandon a team member.

In most cases the conditions and circumstances decide it for you, and this time was no exception, but it doesn't lessen the terrible nature of what you are forced to do. We detached the rope and made the rest of the descent painfully slowly. Even at this stage it was still in my mind that we would be able to seek help once we got down, but I think I was reassuring myself rather than expecting rescue to be likely. By the time we reached safety we were both in that curious state of partial reality when you know that someone else has now got to take control.

Climbing is a dangerous activity, there are many accidents and deaths and every experienced climber acknowledges this, but this was my friend and close team mate and, for me, there will always be the guilt that I had to leave him there.

***

Miranda involuntarily took a deep breath and considered what she had read. Duncan's recalling of the terrible events was painful to read and made her aware again of her isolation from what had happened to Mike and her regret that she had not been able to get to know his family and friends. One of the hardest things was not being acknowledged as someone who was bereaved. She admired Duncan's integrity and strength of character in his presentation of the events as he had not directly implicated Tom, even though he must have been deeply distressed and angry at the loss of his friend.

Nevertheless she was relieved that Tom had directed her to the article as it provided a sort of closure. It also made her return to her discussion with Susannah and her need to make future plans.

Chapter 19

Jasmin

She began by going to the gallery to look at her work and to discuss her options with Kay and Paul. The icons looked good displayed on the end wall of the gallery: the austerity of the white-painted wall and the carefully angled lighting emphasised their lines and colours. Kate and Paul were pleased with the interest that they had provoked and were optimistic about sales.

'So, what's the next project to be, Miranda?' Paul asked.

'Good question; not sure where to go from here but I do need to think about it.'

And after she left the gallery she did consider this. A lot of things were changing in her life at the moment and it could be a good time to go for a change of direction in her creative work. She had spent so long doing the same range of paintings and drawings inspired by urban scenes, classic architecture and objects that intrigued her. She was a reflective, meditative artist as she was in other aspects of her life and her concern was to suggest abstract concepts through drawings and paintings of buildings and artefacts. She hoped that for her audience she had created mystery, intrigue and ambiguity as characteristics of her depopulated work. But had she, like Beckett with his constant minimising and reducing in his plays, actually drawn herself into a corner. She so loved the drawings of Ruskin and the purity of the still life creations of Morandi that she felt she had been seduced by concentrating on this type of familiar ground. Or did her reluctance to incorporate figures and people stem from her recent intense study of Hammershoi and Munch; the first with his frequent inclusion of the lone figure of his wife in his interior scenes, and Munch with his portrayal of tormented people? Maybe it was time to force herself out of her comfort zone. She had of course studied and practised life drawing and had taught it to students but it had not been a path she chose to follow. It demanded intense concentration and she could recall as a student the frustration of not achieving what she wanted and the physical effect, on occasions, of blinding migraines after a lengthy session. She thought of Anni's skilful, delicate nudes that were gentle and sensual at the same time and of the interesting, clever (if not very flattering sketches) that Max had done of her at the studio. But this now presented itself as a challenge for her professional development.

As a starting point she decided to ask Jasmin to sit for her fully clothed. She liked Jasmin's bone structure and large dark eyes that always looked kohl rimmed and shadowed even when she was not wearing make-up. She would get her to come to the studio and make it into a group session; there would be much more fun if the others wanted to participate. The studio was not sufficiently heated to expect a model to pose naked, and anyway, she was unsure how Jasmin would feel about that. In fact Jasmin was responsive to the idea, not least for the promise of an afternoon spent exploring the streets and stores of Camden Town on a Saturday afternoon.

'It's so different from where I live, Miranda. My home is so stuffy and suburban.'

Miranda organised the structure of the session, beginning with quick timed sketches to loosen up, moving around the room and with Jasmine changing position to achieve different perspectives, and then a longer session of individual drawing with everyone choosing their own materials. Jasmine's patience and calmness made her an excellent model and soon there was an atmosphere of quiet, thoughtful absorption. Miranda loved this; to work alone and yet be aware of others around her engaged in the same task in different ways was oddly satisfying; rather like the experience of being in Vikram's yoga room.

Afterwards she took Jasmin, Rebecca and Max to Marine Ices.

'My treat. You were great, Jasmin and thanks, Rebecca for letting us use the studio.'

'And, what about me?' Max asked. 'What have I done to benefit from your generosity?'

'Oh, just the value of your stimulating company.'

After the inevitable debate about flavours and combinations they ordered ice creams and coffees and chatted about the experience of life drawing.

'You know,' Miranda said. 'I think my reluctance to commit to life drawing goes way back to a class I went to when I was still at school. We had a temporary tutor for one class because our regular one was away or something. The replacement was an unhelpful woman who issued instructions and then toured the room peering over people's shoulders largely without comment. When she got to me she paused and said. "A piece of advice: if I were you I'd engage my brain before I started".'

'How cruel,' Jasmin said. 'No wonder it put you off.'

'The funny thing was that at the end of the session she made us all take our work and line it up against the wall. Naturally, I didn't want to but she took mine and propped it right in the centre, then proceeded to do a serious critique of it: she said it reminded her of Matisse.'

'Yeah, I can see that in the ones you did today of Jasmin,' Max said. 'So there's hope for you yet.'

'And, I'd like to bet,' Rebecca said, 'that she wasn't a successful commercial artist as you are becoming. Did you see any of her work?'

'Well, no, but I'm not successful or even aspiring in the field we're talking about. In fact, we mostly didn't with our tutors; see their work, I mean. That's why I think it's important to continue being a practitioner. How can you teach and advise on a skill that you are not practising yourself?'

'This ice cream is totally fantastic,' Jasmine commented. 'Ice cream is my absolute failing; just as well I don't live here or I'd be indulging every day.'

Then, looking out at the street, she groaned. 'Oh no, one of those Romanian women is hanging round outside.'

There had been a disturbing altercation earlier just before they reached the ice cream parlour. A small group of Romanian women were on the street, spread out at intervals to beg. Some of them carried babies which they thrust into the faces of passers-by as an inducement to pity, while extending a hand for money. One of the women approached their group and targeted Max, holding out one hand and pleading while holding the baby like a bundle in her other arm.

When Max tried to courteously ignore her she became insistent and clutched his jacket. Assuming that this was an attempt to steal his wallet, Miranda intervened to push her away but this just resulted in her transferring her attentions to Miranda instead. The woman was wearing a long thin scarf which at some stage had become twined round Miranda's arm so that they were tied together. The woman herself now seemed to be getting into a state of panic and one of her companions arrived to see what was going on. As she couldn't speak English it was impossible to pacify her and it took Rebecca's assistance to disentangle the mess.

'Leave it, Max,' Rebecca said, when he attempted to help. 'Don't touch her or she might accuse you of attacking her.'

Once the woman had been released and had moved on they were able to see the amusing side of what had been an unpleasant incident.

'God, I feel quite out of breath,' Miranda said.

'Crazy to think that four of us in broad daylight could have been threatened like that,' Jasmin said.

And now they were back and hanging around outside the cafe.

'I think I must attract that kind of attention,' Miranda said as she recalled the episode with the gypsy outside the gastropub before the Summer break.

'That one, I think was putting a curse on me. And sometimes I think it must have worked considering a few of the things that have happened recently.'

'You know, there could be something in that, Max was saying. I mean, did you know that in Romania being a witch is an accepted occupation; apparently it's part of the culture.'

'How do you know?' Rebecca asked. 'I thought your travelling abroad was mostly limited to the Cote D'Azur and swanky places. Can't see you following the Dracula trail.'

'Oh, like most of my knowledge it's acquired from newspapers. Apparently they (the witches, that is), have been protesting against new tax laws whereby witches, fortune tellers and astrologers will have to pay sixteen per cent of their income in tax.'

'No! Jasmin said. 'Would this have been April first when you read it?'

'No, seriously, it's true. The Romanian government do take these occupations seriously and even wear purple on certain days to ward off evil.'

'OK, so what do they do?' Miranda asked. 'Cast spells?'

'Yes, actually. They make potions using cat excrement and the bodies of dead dogs and hurl poisonous mandrake plants into the Danube. They are threatening to bring down the government.'

'Oh, that is gross,' Jasmin said. 'Although we could do with one of their spells to cast against Morticia and the Prince of Darkness at college.'

Warming to the topic, Max said. 'There's even a head witch called Alisia who's leading the protest.'

'Well, we wouldn't need witches' spells to bring down our government,' Rebecca commented. 'They're doing a pretty good job of it themselves with their lies and general incompetence.'

'And what's the significance of the colour purple?' Miranda queried.

'The witches can attack you with negative energy and wearing purple clothing supposedly makes the wearer superior and wards off evil.'

'Well, that would seem to be the obvious answer,' Jasmin said. 'Just wear purple all the time.'

'Meanwhile, before we leave, could anyone manage another ice cream? I'm determined to indulge myself today.'

Rebecca was persuaded into sharing one and Max and Miranda settled for more coffee.

It was dusk by the time they left Marine Ices. The women were nowhere to be seen but as Max said goodbye to them in turn he said to Miranda. 'Have a good evening but I suggest you don't choose "Macbeth" as your bedtime reading.'

Miranda had a resurgence of interest in her artwork. It was good to draw back from her studies of Munch and Hammershoi and her work for the gallery. The life drawing was about developing her skills without the pressure of promoting or selling it. She set up an easel in her living room near the window to benefit from the light and, using the room as a focal point, began to create her own painting. The backdrop to her composition was to be a shuttered window, rather like those in a French chateau. The shutters were drawn back and there was a vague suggestion of an exterior, possibly an overgrown garden. There was an ornamental cornice and carvings in the plasterwork on the walls and a door to the left of the window gave a limited view of a corridor.

The central focus of the painting was a female figure, apparently asleep on a chaise longue with her face half buried in cushions and long fair hair cascading over her shoulders. She was slim and naked except for a sheet of some cream coloured fabric which was loosely draped over her. There was an anklet on one of her legs which Miranda added to give some intrigue, perhaps an implication of slavery or possession? She was enjoying playing around with the mystique of the scene and wanted it to prompt questions about the narrative behind it. The colours on her palette were changing with this painting; she was working with gouache in earthy washes and softer shades of yellowy orange, burnt sienna and ochre. At moments like this she felt peacefully at one with her work. The telephone interrupted her concentration. It was Jasmin's soft, quiet voice.

'Hi Jasmin, this is a pleasant surprise.'

'Sorry for disturbing you.' (Jasmin was always politely apologetic.)

'No, you're not.'

'But I wondered if you'd be free after college tomorrow to go for a coffee with me.'

'Yeah, sure that would be nice but I thought you usually went straight home unless Jamal met you.'

'Mm, but there's something I want to ask you.'

'I'm intrigued.' Miranda laughed.

But Jasmin was reluctant to elaborate and wanted to go. She seemed breathless.

'OK, that's great. Meet you in your room when we finish tomorrow.'

They chose one of the coffee shops in the glitzy St Pancras concourse. Miranda loved being here; watching people leaving and arriving on Eurostar. In fact, all large transport hubs gave her a sense of anticipation, even if she was not travelling herself.

'Why the change of routine,' Miranda asked?

Jasmin looked diffident as she fiddled with her coffee cup.

'Oh, I told Jamal there was a college meeting. Look, Miranda, I'd like to ask you a favour.'

'Yes, of course,' Miranda said (although wondering why she automatically agreed without knowing what the favour was).

'Next weekend, can I tell Jamal that I'm staying at your flat?'

'Well, you can stay if you want to, but why?'

'Thing is, I want to go away for the weekend without him and need an excuse.'

'But what's the reason? If you're going off with one of your sisters somewhere why not just tell him? Surely he'd be OK with that?'

'Yes, but ... Jasmin was becoming increasingly self conscious. No, it's not a girls' shopping weekend. I'm meeting someone.'

'You mean, a guy?' Miranda couldn't believe what she was hearing.

'Yes. I think I'm in love.'

Stunned wasn't enough to describe the shock this gave Miranda. Even though she found the arranged marriage concept extraordinary she had been so impressed with Jasmin's account of the arrangements and the affection she had shown for Jamal that she had wanted it to work. For a while she was silent, looking at Jasmin's pleading eyes until she had to force herself to respond.

'I don't know what to say; I thought you were such a devoted couple.'

'We are, I mean we were but then recently I realised how oppressive he is and how he dominates my life. He has to know what I am doing all the time and he won't let me go anywhere unless he's with me, except for a few hours with my sisters or female friends like you. When you invited me to your private view he said he had to come with me if I was going to get all dressed up and go to a place where there were men I didn't know.'

'And you looked so great together,' Miranda said sadly, remembering the evening vividly.

But now that the outpouring had started, Jasmin just continued.

'He's not even that interested in Art, but he is obsessed with where I am, what I'm doing, what I'm wearing, who I'm with.'

'I certainly understand that's a problem, but it didn't seem to bother you before.'

'That was before I met Raj.'

'Raj? Who is he? Is he Muslim? How on earth did you meet him?' There were now so many questions.

'It was at a family party; he is a friend of one of our cousins. And, yes, he is Muslim.'

'But again,' (Miranda was remembering what Jasmin had told her about her customs and lifestyle).

'Surely you can't be alone in a room with a man that you don't know?'

'Oh, we weren't. It wouldn't be possible to be alone at these gatherings; there are people everywhere talking, eating. It's like Bedlam,' she laughed. 'This is how it happened. There was a group of us sitting talking and he kept catching my eye and I knew there was something there.'

'So, it was love at first sight?' Miranda asked, wondering if Jasmin had exchanged an arranged marriage for a fantasy.

'I guess so. And then, at the end of the evening he said quietly "text me your number".'

'How on earth do you expect to get away with this? If Jamal is so jealous has it occurred to you that he probably checks your phone?'

'Oh, he does sometimes but now I switch it off when I'm in the house and I don't use it in front of him.'

'Don't you feel that you're being dishonest with Jamal? Wouldn't it be better to tell him?'

'No, it's OK for you to say that. You're a free spirit compared to me. He'd go insane and our families would get involved.'

'Well, that in a way makes it worse. You're taking a hell of a risk. This could be dangerous.'

'I know, but I have to do it. How have you felt when you've been in love? All I can do is think about Raj. I want to be with him and I get worked up at the prospect of seeing him. The worst part about this is when love turns to hate. All the things I loved about Jamal I loathe now.'

'Like?' Miranda asked.

'Oh, the way he's so organised and pedantic about everything, his obsessive tidiness, fussing about food, always wanting to see everything I've bought when I've been shopping (and that's on the rare occasions when I go without him). When we first got married I thought he wanted to be with me all the time and share things but now I see he's a total control freak. Everything he does irritates me, all his personal habits. I even detest the way he eats.' And she burst out laughing. 'He chomps on his food and when we have a traditional meal he always mops up the sauce with naan bread.'

'Well, yeah, but lots of us do that,' Miranda said. For some reason she found herself actually defending Jamal but Jasmin ignored her.

'You know, I looked at him over the breakfast table this morning and thought "Do I even like you?"'

So, will you help me? Can I say that I'm staying with you?'

Although still astonished at Jasmin's revelations, Miranda considered the practicalities.

'Wouldn't he use your mobile anyway and then he wouldn't know where you were?'

'Yes, but he'd insist on knowing where I would be and having a landline number to check.'

'Oh great, so if he rings my landline what do I say when he asks to speak to you?'

'Just say I'm in the shower or something and then I'll call him back.'

'Except how can you call him back if you're not with me?'

'If he rings I'd like you to call me and then I'll phone him back on my mobile.'

'God, this was getting complicated,' Miranda thought.

'And what exactly are we supposed to be doing on this weekend.'

'A public art exhibition in a gallery near you. Like I said, he's not keen on contemporary art and if he thinks it's just us he'll trust me. He really likes you, Miranda.'

'Well, he definitely won't if he finds out.'

'The other reason for asking you is that he may mention it next time he sees you.'

'In that case, I'll do my best to make sure that I don't have a conversation with him if we should happen to meet.'

Jasmin looked delighted and, Miranda had to admit, her eyes were sparkling and she looked as attractive as Miranda had ever seen her.

Checking the time, she rushed to collect her things.

'Go to go, or I will be facing the inquisition.'

When Jasmin had rushed off Miranda bought another coffee and sat for a while to think this through. Was she upset that her illusions had been destroyed, anxious about being involved in the deception and concerned for Jamin's safety?

Yes, all of those things but worse, she actually felt envious of Jasmin's excitement and happiness. It reminded her so much of the wave of euphoria that she had felt with Mike. How she missed both him and those feelings.

Over the next few weeks she saw the change in Jasmin. She was talkative, faster in her speech and seemed unable to concentrate. She had lost weight and played with her food or avoided eating. Almost as if she was on amphetamines, Miranda thought: 'but wasn't being in love the same?' She recalled her own intoxicating early days with Mike and the constant surges of energy. But, in Jasmin's case there was the potential for real danger. She confided in Miranda that she was taking every opportunity to meet Raj, sneaking out to meet him when Jamal was attending evening lectures and even inventing a late class at college that she claimed she had been asked to teach. He seemed to accept the excuses, including a couple of Saturday nights when again Miranda was the alibi. For her part, Miranda knew that she was taking a vicarious interest, or even pleasure, in Jasmin's affair and on the occasions when she did see Jamal waiting for Jasmin after college she limited any contact to a quick greeting. He did call Miranda's landline one Saturday evening and asked to speak to Jasmin as he couldn't get a response from her mobile but when Miranda offered the excuse of Jasmin taking a shower he said 'No problem' and simply asked if she would pass on a message from Jasmin's sister about an invitation for the next day. Miranda called Jasmin's mobile to alert her to Jamal's message. She could tell from her voice that she was in the hotel room with Raj and was curiously indifferent to the call. Miranda was angry at being drawn into the deception and the fact that she was actually scared for Jasmin while Jasmin herself was remarkably unconcerned.

But it was not to last. It was a Saturday evening in the packed wine bar: Miranda was enjoying a drink with Camden friends after being solitary for some time. There were comments about her at last coming out of hibernation and she was enjoying the attentions of a guy called Steve who was a friend of one of the regulars. She was suddenly aware of several missed calls on her phone and an answerphone message. It was Jasmin, distressed and sobbing. 'Miranda, can you call me. Don't know what to do?' Fearing that Jamal had found out Miranda returned the call.

'Jasmin, where are you? Are you OK?'

'I'm at the hotel where I was supposed to meet Raj but he hasn't turned up and I've been calling his mobile for hours. I can't call him at home because he lives in his parents' house.'

'There really isn't anything you can do, Jasmin. You'll have to leave it until he contacts you. What are you going to do now?'

'I can't go home because Jamal will want to know why and I don't want to stay here on my own.'

'Do you want to stay at my flat for the night?'

Inevitably the answer was 'yes' so Miranda had to abandon her night out and what was promising to be an interesting conversation with Steve.

Jasmin took a taxi to Miranda's flat to avoid meeting anyone she knew and Miranda reluctantly left the company of her friends and walked home. Oblivious to the inconvenience she was causing to Miranda all Jasmin wanted to do was to tearfully talk about Raj and what might have happened to him. Once Miranda had Jasmin sitting down with a box of tissues and a strong coffee she went into the kitchen to open a bottle of wine.

'Jasmin, I'm going to have a drink.'

No need to be apologetic now for offending Jasmin's religious sensibilities when she was in flagrant disregard of the code she lived by. 'Can I get you something to eat?'

'No, but could I have a glass of wine?'

'Sure.' That was unexpected but it was better than drinking alone.

'Jasmin, is this the first time you have drunk alcohol?'

'No. The first night I spent with Raj he persuaded me to have some wine and after that we always took a bottle up to our room.'

The wine had the desired effect of calming Jasmin and after they had finished the bottle and shared a plate of cheese and biscuits she was exhausted. Miranda arranged the futon in the spare room and stayed up working on her painting for a few hours as she knew that sleep wouldn't come quickly.

At college the next week Jasmin spoke to Miranda quietly during a coffee break in the faculty room.

'I managed to speak to Raj eventually.'

'And?' Miranda queried.

'He said he was sorry but he didn't come because he had to attend a family function and couldn't give a suitable excuse.'

'But God, Jasmin, he could at least have called you.'

'Yes, but that's not all. He said he can't see me again and we have to finish it because he's going to Pakistan to meet a girl that his parents want him to marry. She is a cousin.'

'That's appalling. He's an adult: he's what, late twenties, and he lets his parents push him around. How dare he treat you like that?' Miranda was furious on Jasmin's behalf.

'I know, but I've been a fool. I don't know what I expected. He never offered me anything except the excitement. There was no discussion of a future together but I just wish he'd had the courage to tell me. The way he did it, leaving me alone in that hotel room: it made me feel so sordid.'

'So what happens now?' Miranda asked.

'Nothing. I'll stay with Jamal. I'm sure he never guessed anything.'

Chapter 20

Susannah

She met Susannah in a Pizza Express near the British Museum. It was one of Miranda's non-college days and she had spent some time wandering round the exhibitions in the Museum before making her way to one of the narrow streets between the British Museum and High Holborn. The pizza place was in a restored building which retained an original feature of contemporary stained glass windows. They ordered and Susannah took a pencil and notepad from her bag.

'OK. Let's do it. We'll make a list of pros and cons of whether you should stay or go. Why do you want to leave London? We'll start with the pros first.'

Miranda considered briefly.

'Right. Well, number one problem is college; things aren't going to improve for me there and I've got to get away from Morticia and the Prince of Darkness.'

'Yeah, OK. Susannah said. And ...?'

'Then there's Mike: I'm still trying to come to terms with the fact that he isn't here any more. At first I thought I wanted to meet someone else but recently I had dates with a couple of guys and they were just so boring. Couldn't think of anything to say to them and just wanted my own company. I did like the film guy I met in Lisbon, James. He wasn't like Mike but he was good company and, sort of kind and considerate but in an amusing way.'

'Any other reasons, Susannah continued?'

'Yes, the people I know are changing their lifestyles; I'm pleased that Anni is out of my life but she was part of the whole social scene I was in and that seems to be disintegrating.'

Susannah was thoughtful.

'You know, this reminds me of the list I made for myself when I'd finished my PhD, and then I took off and did some travelling around northern Italy.'

'I thought you was very organised about this,' Miranda said. 'So, why did you do it?'

'I was in Toronto. I'd met William; he was there on a temporary lectureship. We'd gotten involved but he didn't want to commit so I decided to take off and see some of Italy.'

'And was it a good decision?'

'Sure. I loved exploring all that Renaissance art and just being able to make decisions to go someplace without anyone else to consider. She glanced down at her notepad.'

'Have we got to the end of the list of pros?'

'Well, there is the money thing. It's not much of a reason but I can't afford to live where I am now unless I get another full-time post.'

'And why do that now when this has given you the push that you need?'

'Agreed, and if I take the severance pay from college it would tide me over for a while.'

Susannah smiled and said,

'Are there any reasons not to go?'

'The biggest thing is that usually I love it here and I'm afraid of leaving and then missing it all.'

'So, you get this out of your system and then you can come back and start career chasing again.'

'Or maybe by then I'll be confident enough to go independent and sell more of my own work.'

'Exactly.'

As they sat talking over their pizzas Miranda realised that she had always been waiting for something to happen: to pass exams, to establish a career, to find a permanent satisfying relationship. But now it occurred to her that what she needed to do was to step back and treat each phase of her life as significant in its own right.

'Thanks so much for the advice, Susannah. Looks like we've cracked it. Let's have another glass of wine.'

'Great idea and here's to your future.'

Chapter 21

Leaving

Her internet searches had led her to a group of artists and writers living in Lisbon. They were mainly American and had formed into a casual group to exchange ideas about art and writing, and to share their experiences of living in the city. This in turn led her to a blog posted by some artists who were trying to set-up an informal gallery. It was easy to make contact and from there she gained advice about where to rent cheap rooms or studio flats. The group were all self-sufficient and for a modest rent had acquired small premises in an unfashionable part of town which they were promoting through the local alternative arts scene. Miranda was welcome to join them. She knew that this could be a risk as she had no real idea what they would be like but her only financial contribution would be a share of the rent and it would give her an opportunity to work with a team and to promote her own work. A woman called Ellie recommended that she find a cheap room or apartment in an area called Principe Real. Located in one of Lisbon's many hilly areas, it was a twenty-five minute walk or a short bus ride downtown. As well as being inexpensive it was near the Praca Principe Real which had a small public park with a huge shady cedar tree. Accommodation was both cheaper and more available in the winter months and Miranda chose a room with private facilities in a pensao. That gave her the advantage of having the pension owners on the premises, which could be useful and would be less lonely initially than renting a self-contained apartment.

It would mean not having cooking or laundry facilities but she reckoned there was much she could manage with a kettle and a shower room. There would be cheap places to eat out and to buy food, and she needed reasons to go out and meet people.

There had been the occasional email from James with brief accounts of where he was filming but these were rare and it took him some time to reply to hers. She frequently thought about how much she had enjoyed their encounters in Portugal. He was so unlike Mike: whereas Mike had been all spontaneity and breathless excitement, James was more calm and considerate, and had seemed to be genuinely interested in her life and her ambitions for the future. She hoped that he would contact her once he was back in London working on his TV project but that was a wish that she knew might not be fulfilled.

Meanwhile, her preparations for leaving were well under way. She had found a tenant for her flat and Susannah had helpfully offered to store all her personal possessions plus her cherished chaise longue. She gave her pots to Mary downstairs and took all of her artwork to Rebecca's studio. Both Rebecca and Susannah had been generous with offers of accommodation if she needed to return before the end of the tenancy.

She was steeping herself in novels, set in Lisbon, with the feeling that literature was often the way into the secret places of a city. It was certainly preferable to her recent compulsive reading about climbing.

It was her last day at college and her friends from the faculty were going out with her for a farewell meal. She wanted to keep it uncomplicated and someone had suggested a small, inexpensive Italian place on Chalton Street. Here they ate bowls of pasta with artisan bread and drank some fairly sharp Italian wine. She spent some time talking to Justin who described in detail his house projects and ideas for moving into the interior design business. It often took this sort of social occasion to give the opportunity to really connect with someone you'd worked with for years. She felt again how much she would have liked to get to know him better, and she had to admit that much of that was physical attraction, but he had never shown any interest in her and was apparently living with the woman his colleagues had never met. He had always been scrupulous about keeping a clear division between home and work.

There were presents: Susannah gave her a travel journal and there were some sketchbooks and artists' materials. Jasmin produced a tiny piece of Asian jewellery and a beautiful notebook made from recycled materials including fabric from a sari. She was relieved that Jasmin had reverted to her usual calm self and appeared once more contented with her marriage. It was a happy and sad occasion at the same time. Outside the restaurant there were final embraces and kisses.

The tube tonight, she thought. It was one of those misty late October evenings and would soon be time for bonfires and fireworks. Usually she tended hardly to notice her travelling companions but this evening she found her eyes wandering over the people sitting opposite her. There was a young guy in the usual 'don't mess with me' uniform of baggy, low slung jeans and trainers but there was a bizarre note to this garb as he was also wearing a hallowe'en mask. The woman two seats from him, was completely enclosed in a burka. She tried to imagine what it felt like to wear one of those all-enveloping garments. She had read that in poorer homes with limited accommodation they were hung in the hallway near the kitchen where they retained all the cooking odours. How repulsive to walk around all day in a suffocating shroud that reeked of cooking fat. She began to feel uncomfortable; the air in the carriage was stale and fetid. That was the problem with the underground, Ok as long as you didn't think about it, but once you let your mind wander to the possibility of breakdowns or terrorist attacks it became threatening and scary. She was out of her seat and at the door well before it reached the stop. She was relieved to get out. At this time of night the exit from the tube station was not too busy so it was surprising when someone pushed her as she exited the barrier.

Even more so when a soft voice said,

'sorry, oh Miranda, hi.'

Joel.

Not him; not tonight when she had been so euphoric.

For once he deliberately made eye contact with her and, surprisingly, tried to initiate conversation.

'Been out somewhere nice?' he asked.

What would have been a friendly passing question from an acquaintance made her feel distinctly wary and nervous when it was Joel. However, it was a polite enough question and difficult to avoid answering him.

'I have, actually. And what are you doing here?'

'Oh, I live here now. Got a house share nearby; think it's round the corner from where you live.' And then a sly look came over his face as he said.

'So I'll see you around.'

'Not for much longer,' she thought as he walked off. She was going to Portugal next week and with luck would never see him again.

Heathrow Airport

Her flight was early morning so she stayed the night before in a modest airport hotel. It was good to do this, she felt, as it was like part of the journey and already she'd made the break with her old life.

In the hotel that night she reflected on the things that had happened to her in the last year. Her life, usually relatively stable and well planned, had been thrown into turmoil. The chain of events sparked off by Joel's attack had spiralled out of control and had, in effect, cost her her job. Mike's death had been a shattering blow and the strangeness of her relationship with Anni had left her feeling wary about forming such an intense friendship again. Even the haven of peace she thought she had made for herself in the Camden flat had been disrupted by the presence of Toby and Jenny, and the way in which she had involuntarily been drawn into their problems.

But there had also been many positives: her success in selling the triptych, her pleasure at seeing the icons displayed in Paul and Kate's gallery, and the true friendship and support of Susannah. Her time in Lisbon had been inspirational and she felt confident that her creativity could flourish in that environment. And there was James, of course. She wondered how their relationship might have progressed if she hadn't been forced to leave Portugal so soon after meeting him.

The hotel had a buffet-style restaurant where she ate a simple salad with a glass of wine and read her Portuguese phrase book. All that remained was to be ready for the shuttle bus in the morning.

Going back to her room she was organising her things for the next day when her phone signalled a message.

James, 'Hi, how are you. Back in London now and hope we can meet again. Would love to see you. When are you free?'

THE END

About Mary Jay

Mary Jay was born in Newcastle upon Tyne and studied English Literature in Manchester before a career as a tutor in Sixth Form Colleges. She now works as an Education Consultant and is a Senior Examiner for A Level examinations.

Her published work includes textbooks and articles and reviews for teaching publications.

Her interest in art and her love of London provided some of the inspiration for this, her debut novel.

Mary Jay lives in the Cheshire town of Knutsford with her husband and two beautiful Birman cats.

If you have enjoyed Mary Jay's work, please pay it forward and leave a review!

Connect with Mary Jay

Goodreads:

www.goodreads.com/book/show/17617084-deception

Twitter:

@maryjay_jay

Facebook:

www.facebook.com/mary.jay.965580

www.ingramcontent.com/pod-product-compliance
Lightning Source LLC
Chambersburg PA
CBHW062010170626
46813CB00001B/99